MW01077347

STEPHANIE ROWE

Wrapped Up in You

A *Mystic Island* novel

WRAPPED UP IN YOU (*Mystic Island #1*)

For further information, please contact:
Stephanie@stephanierowe.com

Dedication

For my mom. I love you!

Acknowledgements

Special thanks to my beta readers and the Rockstars. You guys are the best! There are so many to thank by name, more than I could count, but here are those who I want to called out specially for all they did to help this book come to life: Malinda Davis Diehl, Donna Bossert, Leslie Barnes, Kayla Bartley, Alencia Bates Salters, Alyssa Bird, Jean Bowden, Shell Bryce, Kelley Daley Curry, Ashley Cuesta, Denise Fluhr, Sandi Foss, Valerie Glass, Heidi Hoffman, Jeanne Stone, Rebecca Johnson, Dottie Jones, Janet Juengling-Snell, Deb Julienne, Bridget Koan, Felicia Low, Phyllis Marshall, Suzanne Mayer, Erin McRae, Jodi Moore, Ashlee Murphy, Judi Pflughoeft, Carol Pretorius, Kasey Richardson, Caryn Santee, Summer Steelman, Nicole Telhiard, Regina Thomas, and Linda Watson. Special thanks to my family, who I love with every fiber of my heart and soul.

Wrapped Up in You

1

COLE CHARBONNEAU FLIPPED up the collar of his overcoat and hunched his shoulders, shielding himself against the driving winds as he studied the woman he'd inadvertently followed onto the main deck of the ferry.

Well, not entirely inadvertently. He'd already been planning to ditch the other passengers in the heated lounge and go solo on deck, but when he'd seen her dark brown hair and long legs disappear up the front stairs, heading out into a bitter Maine wind that she wasn't remotely dressed for...he'd decided to follow her instead of going out the rear door.

She had city-girl written all over her, completely unprepared for the storm raging outside. Her thin leather shoes would never suffice as footwear once she got off the boat onto Mystic Island, and her light blue jacket was more appropriate for a summer evening than late December in northern Maine on a ferry.

When he was a teen, Cole and his buddies used to make a point of providing local "tour guide" services to the girls who vacationed on the island with their families. An out-of-towner like her would have been ripe game to acquire a hormonal escort who was tanned and footloose.

But he wasn't a kid anymore, and the last thing he wanted right now was a woman. Not to mention, he'd worked hard to sever all his ties to the island, so the fact she was riding a ferry headed right toward his old home was enough to make him turn away.

But she was heading out into bad weather she wasn't prepared for, and he wasn't enough of an ass to let her do it alone.

It might have been over a decade since he'd been a regular on this ferry, but it would never be long enough to forget what a winter storm could do to the unprepared. And the ocean? He swore, his mind going to memories he'd managed to forget for a long time.

He dragged his thoughts from a past that could never be changed, and focused on the woman in front of him as he stepped outside. She was leaning on the railing, staring out across the water, her thick curls whipping around her face in the wind. Her cheeks and nose were already red from the cold, but there was an obstinate set to her jaw, one that spoke of a determination to endure the weather and stay where she was, rather than retreat to the enclosed hold down below.

He appreciated the fact she wasn't overly thin, like most of the women he met in New York. He liked the way she filled out her jeans. She had curves, and she didn't bother to hide them. To his surprise, he found himself grinning as he watched her wrap her arms around her torso, fighting a losing battle to retain body heat. She was stubborn. Sexy, stubborn, and apparently somewhat antisocial, given the fact that she'd rejected the heated passenger lounge below deck, complete with Christmas lights, holiday music, and locally brewed eggnog.

He smiled, and strolled across the deck, angling himself easily as the boat canted to the side, tossed by the surging storm tides. The woman lunged for the railing, her fingers sliding off the metal rivets as she tried to hold on. He had no doubt her hands were too cold to grip tightly, and he edged over to her, close enough to grab her if she lost her balance.

Carefully watching to make sure she wasn't in danger of pitching headfirst over the railing into the sea, Cole leaned on the rail beside her. "Nice day," he said conversationally, staring across the surly ocean.

She snapped a sharp look at him, clearly startled to see him. "Oh, um, hi."

"Hi." He turned so he was facing her, resting his elbow on the railing as he studied her. "So, tell me why a woman dressed for summer has rejected the heat and come up here, where your fate is fluctuating between freezing to death or being pitched over the side into the water?"

Her eyes widened, showcasing eyes that might be the richest shade of brown Cole could recall ever seeing. He was riveted by them, deep brown pools of emotion and vulnerability. Her gaze was so intense that he felt like he was falling into it...it felt like the only place he wanted to be. Her lashes were thick and long, framing her eyes like feather-soft whispers. She wore no makeup at all. It was simply her, natural, vulnerable, and sexy as hell. A sudden rush of desire crashed through him, hitting him so hard and so fast that he lost his breath for a split second.

Swearing, he looked away, trying to control the lust thundering through him. What the hell? He never reacted like this to a woman. Ever. Especially now, when he'd sworn off women for the foreseeable future, especially one headed toward his old home.

"Are you always this direct?" she asked, grabbing the railing as the boat tilted again, drawing his attention back to her.

"Yep. Saves time." He cocked his head, studying her, trying to figure out why he was reacting the way he was. There was something about her that drew him in, something that ignited a need to protect her, and a desire to encircle her wrist with his fingers, coax her over to him, and kiss her until neither one of them could think. He felt like she belonged with him, to him, and him to her...but why? He narrowed his eyes, scanning her face, his gaze settling on her expressive, dark eyes again. It was her eyes that had ensnared him...almost as if there was already a connection between them...as if they already knew each other. He frowned, noting her thick hair, the slant of her nose, the way her lips curved. She looked vaguely familiar. "Do I know you?" She looked about his age, maybe a little younger.

Fear flashed across her face, but it was gone almost before he'd seen it. She lifted her chin in that stubborn set he already recognized. "I am sure I would recall if we'd met," she said, with a slight edge of iciness, just enough to let him know to back off...and just enough to make him realize that she was hiding something.

So, he *had* met her before? When? He searched his memories, but the answer slipped out of his grasp, elusive and fleeting.

The ferry pitched sideways, angling up the side of a substantial wave. Cole braced himself, not even bothering to hold onto anything for support, but she lunged for the railing and gripped fiercely. It had been well over a decade since he'd ridden this ferry, but the skills he'd acquired for the first eighteen years of his life hadn't waned with disuse.

He shoved his hands in his pockets, hunching his shoulders against the cold, feigning nonchalance even as he angled himself into the right position to grab her if she was in danger of going over. "We *do* know each other, don't we?" he asked. "How?"

Ignoring his subtle heroic tendencies and his inquiry, she turned her back on him, facing the ocean again. "I'm sure we haven't met," she said succinctly. The message was clear that she wanted to be left alone.

He could respect her wishes and go back inside, where he didn't want to be.

Or he could ignore them and interfere where he wasn't wanted.

He was more in the mood to deal with a hostile, anti-social female than he was to deal with well-wishers who would want to welcome him back to the land he'd walked away from, so, yeah, he was going to stay in her personal space, and that was how it was. Plus, he wanted to know why the hell he was responding to her like he was, a question he suspected she had the answer to.

The boat plummeted sharply down the wave, and she lost her grip, sliding across the deck toward the bow of the ship. He leapt across the deck and caught her arm just before she slammed into the steel siding. She grabbed his wrist with her free hand, bracing her feet as he pulled her to her feet.

The boat pitched again, and he locked his arm around her waist, hauling her against him as he grabbed the railing, fighting to keep both of them balanced. Her body was warm and soft against his, and for a split second, everything inside him went utterly still, completely focused on the feel of her body against his. She stared up at him, not trying to get away, her dark eyes searching his as if she were trying to ferret out the same answers eluding him.

He touched her jaw, sliding his fingers along her skin. "Who are you?" he asked softly. "Who are you to me?"

She shook her head once. "No one," she whispered. "Please, just let it be no one."

The boat dipped, and even he had to take a step to keep their balance. Swearing under his breath, he knew that he couldn't deny the storm anymore. "Inside," he shouted above the wind. "It's getting too dangerous out here." Not dangerous for the ferry, but a little dicey to be standing outside on the deck that was getting increasingly slippery.

"I'm good out here," she retorted, leaning into him for support. She ducked her head, using his chest to shield her face from the wind...and from his inspection. "It's just another hour, right?"

"You'll be dead in an hour," he observed. "Your shoes are worth shit out here." The boat leveled briefly, and he guided her back toward the center of the deck, away from the edges.

"My shoes are fine, and no one dies on these things," she scoffed as she twisted out of his grasp. She sat down on the deck and leaned back against the life preserver container, using it for support. It was a five-foot high container bolted to the deck. She pulled her knees against her chest and wrapped her arms around them. "It's an adventure."

"You think it's an adventure?" He crouched in front of her, unable to suppress his need to protect her. It was intense, powerful, and unyielding. It was personal. Somehow, someway, she was personal to him, and that raised the stakes to a level he couldn't ignore. "Someone I loved died on this ocean in a storm like this one when I was seventeen. It happens. Don't ignore the risks, because they're real." His voice was taut, edged with the strain of memories he'd worked hard to forget, a past that had ruthlessly surged back the moment he'd arrived at the docks, memories which had been mounting every minute since he'd driven his car on board.

She looked up sharply at his words, and for a split second, he forgot about the storm, the boat, and a girl he'd failed so long ago. Instead, he was swept up into eyes so full of emotion that he felt his own heart constrict. Her lashes were clumped from the dampness, her skin the color of the damp beach sand after a storm, her hair a turbulent mass of dark curls framing her face. She looked wild and disheveled, as if the storm itself had borne her onto the deck of the ferry. She was riveting, not just her appearance, but the depth of concern and empathy in her eyes seemed to reach inside him and twist at something that he'd kept shut away for so long.

"I'm sorry," she said softly, putting her hand on his arm. "I'm so sorry."

The feel of her touch was a shock to his system. Grabbing her to keep her from falling off the ferry had been intense, but to have her initiate contact sent all his senses into overdrive. Heat pierced through him, and he went still, unwilling to do anything that would dislodge her touch, or make her look away. He was riveted by the expression on her face, by the way she looked at him as if she saw through all his crap and saw the ache in his chest that haunted him every minute of every day. "Thank you," he said, his voice lower and rougher than he'd intended.

Again, something passed between them, but this time, it was more dangerous, more intense, and more intimate. She swallowed, not breaking physical contact or taking her gaze off his.

The boat pitched again, and he braced his hand on the wall above her head to keep his balance, a position that brought him further into her space, looming over her. It put him between her and the storm, and he liked being there, her protector. In the alcove beside the container, it was quieter, and he didn't have to shout. "It was a long time ago," he acknowledged.

She cocked her head, studying him. "Not long enough," she observed.

"No," he said softly. "Never long enough to forget."

They stared at each other, and for a third time, something shifted between them, an understanding, a moment of connection in the midst of a storm that held no mercy for those in its path. He knew in that moment that he was lost to her, to the woman whose name he didn't even know, who was nothing more than a moment in the midst of a rising storm. "I'm Cole Charbonneau," he said.

She hesitated, and he saw a flicker of doubt on her face. "Kate Smith," she said quickly, too quickly.

That wasn't her real name.

She'd lied to him.

Denial roared through him, a repudiation of her

withdrawal. He wanted to slide his hand behind her head and draw her to him, eradicating the distance she'd just erected between them. "I don't believe you," he said softly, leaning closer. "Your name isn't Kate Smith, is it?"

Her eyes widened, and he saw a flash of fear in her eyes. Fear of being identified? Shit. Her insistence on hiding on deck instead of in the lounge with the other passengers suddenly made sense. Who was she hiding from? He wanted to ask. He needed to know. He burned to fix it. He instinctively looked over his shoulder, scanning the deck for the threat she was hiding from. He saw no one, but that didn't ease the sudden rush of energy pouring through him, the need to protect her, to use his body as a shield to keep her safe.

Her eyes widened, and she shook her head. "It's Kate Smith," she said again, giving him an unabashed stare as she lied again, her jaw jutting out in defiance. "Don't try to invent things that don't exist."

Her warning hung between them, a cold knife that sliced through the heat that had been building. His jaw flexed in frustration, and he felt himself shutting down, pulling back.

What the hell was he doing, obsessing over her? This island and its people weren't his world anymore. The ferry was taking him to the place he'd left behind so long ago, and this was the very last time he'd ever set foot on that soil. Whoever Kate Smith was, if she was a part of Mystic Island, he wasn't getting involved.

"Fine. You're Kate Smith." He sat down beside her and draped his arms over his knees. He ground his jaw and leaned his head back against the side of the container, moodily glaring at the turbulent sky.

She stared at him. "You're staying here?"

"Yes, I am. Not because I'm trying to invent anything between us, but because I have no interest in being inside. I hate eggnog, and everything related to Christmas, so up here is better."

For a long moment, she said nothing. She just stared at him. He tensed, ready for her to push back, to try to get him to retreat. But after a moment, she leaned back against the container again, settling in beside him, not touching, but close to him.

As they sat there, some of his tension began to ease. He watched Kate out of the corner of his eye, noticing the sadness in her eyes, and the lines at the corners of her mouth. He realized she was like a wild animal, pushing back when he'd cornered her. He understood that, because he'd been there too. He wondered again what she was hiding from. How bad was it?

He sighed as the last vestiges of his irritation with her faded, drifting away in the blustery wind, replaced by a feeling of camaraderie, two people who would rather freeze their asses off than socialize below deck. "Snow's coming. It's going to be a rough one."

She was starting to shiver, and he contemplated what to do about it.

She looked across the water. "I like snow."

"You'd better. This one's going to knock the town on its ass tonight." He wedged his feet against a second storage bin, locking himself in place. "Want my coat?"

She glanced at him. "Yes," she said, with a candor that he appreciated. "But then you'll freeze…unless you're going back inside and won't need it," she added with a hopeful edge to her voice.

He grinned at her attempt to discourage him. "Sorry. I'm staying. Out here is better." Better because he didn't have to talk to people who knew him. Better because, after fending off superficial women in his real life, Kate Smith and her elusiveness interested him. And better, because he wanted to be outside with her in case the storm became more than she could handle. His failure to act had left one person dead during a storm like this, and there was no chance he was going to make the same mistake again. He was a hell of a lot stronger and bigger than Kate was, and he could handle the pitches better. And if it got too bad, he was going to make her go inside, no matter what she wanted.

"Oh." She looked so crestfallen, he actually laughed.

"So, since you won't take my coat, how about we negotiate?" He raised his arm, making space for her to tuck herself against him inside his heavy coat. "Compromise?"

She glanced at him, biting her lip with apparent trepidation. Then the boat pitched again, and she started to slide across the deck away from him. She immediately lunged for him. He caught her arm and helped her get back to him. She nestled up against his side, and he wrapped his coat around them both, locking Kate against him.

She scooted closer, burying her trembling body in his heat. She said nothing as she wedged herself against him, wrapping her fingers around the edge of his coat to pull it even more tightly around her. Neither of them commented, but the intimacy of the situation was visceral and intense. He tightened his arm around her, pulling her even closer against him. She snuggled herself against him even more, her shoulders wedged under his arm. When she sighed and leaned her head against his chest, surrendering to the situation, rightness roared through him. He didn't know her, but at the same time, he *knew* her, and he wanted her right where she was.

She was so vulnerable, awakening a long-buried need to protect, one that he hadn't acknowledged in a long time.

He didn't want to be that guy again.

He didn't want to be headed toward that island.

He didn't want to revisit the past he'd left behind.

But as Kate snuggled more tightly against his side, he realized that he did want one thing: to be right there, in the storm, away from the heated lounge, with a woman who had awakened a primal part of him that he'd forgotten existed, the part that made him feel like he was alive again, the part that made him care.

2

COLE CHARBONNEAU WAS dangerous.

There was no doubt in Willow Morgan's mind that the man she was tucked up against could wreck everything for her. He'd looked at her with far too much shrewdness, and he clearly knew she'd lied about her name.

But he was less of a threat than the lounge full of strangers below deck, all of whom clearly believed that a solo woman on the Mystic Island ferry a week before Christmas was in dire need of having her holiday improved. Less than three minutes after she'd walked into the ferry lounge, she'd had an eggnog in her hand and three inquisitive new best friends wanting to know why on earth she was planning to spend Christmas by herself, on an island where she didn't know a soul.

That kind of social connection was exactly what she'd come here for...and yet it had threatened everything that mattered to her. They would ask questions she didn't want to answer, questions that would make it too easy for them to figure out who she was…and then her trip would fail.

Willow couldn't afford to have it fail. This trip was her last chance to feel like she could breathe again. She'd panicked and fled…and wound up in the arms of a stranger who was dangerous, sexy, and burdened with a past as dark as hers.

Yes, sure, she was being reckless for staying out on the deck in the storm.

She was probably being naive and foolish to hunker down with some guy she didn't know.

But, quite frankly, she didn't care whether she should be out there or not.

She liked being so cold it felt like her insides were going to splinter into a thousand pieces.

She liked being terrified each time the ferry crashed down the side of another wave.

And she really liked burying herself against Cole, letting his strength and warmth wrap around her like an impenetrable shield that would protect her from the risk of hypothermia or drowning.

Being in the blustery air with Cole felt good, not because she was a bold risk-taker, because she wasn't. It was because this moment, this coldness, the wind, the fear, and the comfort of his warmth made her feel alive. She was so scared, so cold, and so touched by his support that there was simply no way to stay dead inside, and that was why she'd come to this island, by herself, for Christmas.

She didn't want to feel dead anymore. She wanted to claw her way back to having her heart beat before it shut down forever. She'd tried everything to heal the cleaving wound in her heart, and nothing had worked.

All she had left was a distant, faded memory of this island from when she was fifteen, the one moment in her life when she'd felt whole, loved, and happy. She was coming back here to try to find that place once again, but this time for real. If she found it, she wasn't going to let it go again.

"So, Kate, do you live on the island?" Cole asked. He was watching the approaching clouds, his dark eyes assessing as he inspected the sky. His voice was deceptively casual, belying the sharp intellect she already knew was there. He was still trying to figure her out, which made her edgy.

She shifted restlessly. "Me? No. I thought you did." She'd thought the island was so small that everyone knew each other, but if Cole lived there, then why had he asked?

"I used to. Not for a long time." The ferry rocked again, and he tightened his arm around her as she started to slide across the slick deck. He was firmly wedged between the two storage containers, but her legs weren't long enough to reach the second one and still have her back against the first. Without him as her anchor, there was no way she'd be able to sit there and not be tossed all over the deck.

"You moved away?" She shifted restlessly, feeling awkward being so wrapped up with him. For heaven's sake, her breasts were practically in his lap. Sitting there silently while her body was smashed up against his was just...awkward. It was too intimate. She needed to create conversation, some sort of connection that would balance the situation out. "Why did you leave the island? Because of the person who died?" Willow grimaced when the question spilled out. She hadn't meant to bring it up. It was clear it was a memory that still hurt, one that he preferred not to address. She was all too familiar with painful memories that needed to be left behind. Excellent. She'd just made an awkward situation even more awkward. That took talent. "I'm sorry. That's none of my business."

"It's okay." He ground his jaw, still staring across the sound. "She was part of the reason I left, but it was bigger than that. I just wanted out."

She frowned at his answer. "I thought it was a wonderful place to live. Why did you want to leave? I've heard about the amazing Christmases they have here. When I was younger..." She paused, not wanting to give any hints that would reveal who she was. "I mean, I've heard people talk about this place. Christmas on the island is special." Was she wrong? That was why she'd come. She would be pretty much devastated if she got off the ferry and found herself stranded for a week in some depressing, worn-out, frigid pile of rocks in the Atlantic Ocean. When she'd come here before, as a fifteen-year-old, it had been summer, and the island had been packed with tourists. What if it was a ghost town in the winter?

He glanced at her, one eyebrow quirking up. "You're here for Christmas? Alone?" He sounded surprised.

She bit her lip and shrugged, stiffening, unable to keep the defensiveness out of her voice. "Yes, so? Don't people come here for Christmas?"

He smiled, and brushed a lock of her hair away from her face. "That they do," he said. "Some people have been coming here for forty years. Every holiday is a big deal on Mystic Island, but Christmas is the biggest. Why are you coming?"

"Because I want to see what it's like." She didn't

really feel like going into the details with him. She didn't want to admit that she was hoping that finding the magic of Christmas would somehow heal her soul. She tried to direct the conversation away from herself and her reasons for coming to the island. "What about the other holidays? Is Mystic Island really magic?"

"Magic?" He sighed, pulling his coat tighter around them. "Many dreams have come true on Mystic Island. Legend says that the island will claim certain people upon their arrival, and it won't let them leave until they find what they came for."

Her heart skipped a beat, and hope rushed through her. She sat up and turned toward him, searching his face. "Is it true? Is that legend true? How does the island keep people from leaving? How does it decide who to claim?"

He looked over at her, his eyebrows going up. "The ferry comes only once a week during the winter," he said. "It's easy to have something go wrong. There was one man who couldn't leave the island for fifty years, according to the stories."

"Really?" Her heart started to race. She wanted to be claimed by the island, to be held captive until her heart became whole again. "What did he come for?"

"I don't know what he came for, but it was love that he got." His eyes seemed to darken as he looked at her. "The island claims people who need love."

"Love?" she echoed, unable to keep the disappointment out of her voice. "He got *love*?"

He looked surprised. "That's the magic of the island. Love. Isn't that what you came for? Christmas love?"

"No! Not love." *Love.* Disappointment surged through her. The last thing she wanted was love. Love was what had broken her. "I just wanted Christmas. You know, glittery lights, home cooked meals, Christmas carols. The spirit of Christmas."

Cole was watching her intently. "You don't want love?"

"No." She bit her lip, tearing her gaze off his to look across the water, hating the emptiness in her chest. She'd once believed in love. She'd fought for it, from her parents first, and then from others. "Love is not worth the effort. Ever."

"Then you better hope the island doesn't claim you."

She looked sharply at him, irritated by his insistence on love. "What about you?" she challenged, wanting the focus of the conversation off of herself and love. "What if it claims you?"

He shrugged. "It can't claim me."

"Why? Because you're native? Or because you're already in love?" The moment she asked the question, her heart skipped a beat. She hadn't even thought of that possibility. What if he had some adoring girlfriend? Or a wife? Oh, *God.* She sat up, pulling away from him, heat burning in her cheeks. How could she be pretzeled up with him if he was already involved with someone?

"Me? In love?" He laughed softly. "No chance of that."

"Oh." She relaxed again. "Then why can't the island claim you?"

He tugged her closer, eliminating the space she'd just put between them. "Because I don't believe."

She snuggled against him, letting his warmth and his scent wrap around her. It felt so right to be in his arms. She'd forgotten what it felt like to be held so securely, to feel safe in a man's embrace. "You don't believe in what? Love?"

"Any of it. Love. Magic. Legends."

"Love can be a terrible thing, but it's real. I believe in it. You don't even believe in love?" When he shook his head, she frowned. "But you're from here. You grew up here, right? Haven't you seen the magic of the island happen?"

"I've seen people think they fall in love plenty of times." He took her hand and ran his fingers over her palm, sending chills down her spine. "But I don't believe the island made it happen, and I don't believe that love exists the way it's presented in fairytales and stories."

"What do you believe in, then?" She was riveted by him, by this private, deep conversation in the middle of a storm with a stranger, talking about death, and love, and magic. She'd spent her entire life being judged, monitoring every word she spoke, knowing that nothing she said or did was ever private. But right now, with Cole, she felt like she was in a secret world, where confessions disappeared into the wind after they were spoken, giving her the freedom to just be, to just say, to just breathe. She watched him run his fingers over her palm, a casual intimacy that felt amazing.

He looked over at her. "I don't believe in anything, anymore," he said quietly.

The stark honesty and lack of emotion in his voice made her heart tighten. "That's what I'm scared of," she admitted. "I'm scared of becoming like that. I don't want to not believe in anything." She couldn't keep the fear out of her voice. "I feel like I'm dying inside, and I don't know how to stop it. I need the magic, Cole. I need the legend of Mystic Island to be true. That's why

I'm here. It has to be true."

He said nothing, his dark gaze searching hers. "I swear I know you," he said softly, lifting a hand to trail it along her jaw. "I remember those eyes. Your voice. It's like..." His finger traced across her skin, sending chills racing down her spine.

She closed her eyes, drinking in the feel of his touch, so light, so sensual, it made her entire body long for more. He was dangerous and mysterious, strong and protective, so erotic that he made her want to embrace her femininity and allow it to flourish, instead of hiding it away.

He moved closer, and she felt his breath against her ear. "Who are you, Kate Smith?" he asked, his voice sending chills down her spine. "Who are you, to me?"

Willow shook her head. "No," she said. "Let me be Kate." She opened her eyes and caught her breath. His face was so close to hers that all he'd have to do was move an inch to kiss her. Adrenaline raced through her. He was so incredibly sexy, in the rough, rugged way of a man bound to the land, a man who lived with honor. "Kiss me," she said suddenly, the words bursting out before she'd even articulated them.

His eyes widened, and she felt her cheeks heat up. "Oh, God," she said, pulling back. "I didn't mean to say that. I don't even know you." She scrambled out from under his arm and lunged to her feet, horrified. Was she that desperate to feel alive that she'd actually asked a complete stranger to kiss her just because he called to her in a way that she hadn't felt in so long? She hadn't felt this kind of connection to anyone for years. The last time she'd felt like this had been the only other time she'd been on the island. It had been only one night, one evening, but she'd never forgotten how she'd felt that night. That was why she was coming back...to find that moment that she'd failed to hold onto so long ago. She was *not* here to beg for kisses from a man she didn't even know. "Never mind—"

Cole stood up, grabbing her wrist as she started to walk away. His dark eyes were burning into her, his jaw hard and angled. He was so male, so intense, so powerful, as if he were carrying the burdens of a thousand civilizations on his shoulders. Was this the man who had confessed his guilt over someone's death only minutes ago? Where was the vulnerability he'd let her see when he'd told her he didn't believe in love. Had she imagined it? She searched his face, looking past the rigidity of his jaw and the taut lines of his mouth, looking for the softness. She tried to imagine his mouth turning up in a smile, his eyes crinkling with laughter...

Recognition suddenly flashed through her mind, and she froze. Dear heavens. She'd seen him smile before. She'd heard him laugh. She *did* know him. He was the boy, the boy from that night so many years ago when she'd been on the island. Her first kiss, in the moonlight, on the beach that had felt endless and beautiful. *It was him.* "Cole?" she whispered in shock. She'd forgotten his name. She'd forgotten what he looked like. All she'd remembered was how he'd made her feel. But it was him. She knew it was.

"Kate." He whispered her fake name, the name she suddenly didn't want to be. Then he pulled her against him, his hand sliding up into her hair as he lowered his head. Her heart hammered when she realized what he was doing. He was giving her what she'd asked for. He was going to kiss her.

Suddenly, all the stakes had changed. He wasn't a

safe, random stranger in a storm. He was real, someone she knew, someone who had mattered to her so long ago. She grabbed his wrist, intending to stop him, but before she could, his lips touched hers, and he kissed her, sweeping her up into the most romantic, most seductive, most dangerous kiss of her life.

She had no chance to stop him, or to keep herself from responding.

3

*H*ER MOUTH TASTED like the ocean air and freedom, mixed with the innocent sensuality of a woman who could bring him to his knees. Cole sank his fingers deeper into Kate's hair as he angled his head, tasting every inch of her lips. Salty. Sweet. Her lips were cold, but decadently soft, and her body felt incredible as she melted against him. He could feel her breasts pressed against his chest, a wildly erotic sensation with the wind whipping around them and the ferry trying to toss them around.

He backed her against the life preserver container, using his body to pin her against the hard plastic while he tunneled his hand through her hair, holding her where he wanted while he deepened the kiss. Her response was intoxicating. She was kissing him back as if she'd been waiting for his kiss her entire life. His cock rose hard and fast, straining against his jeans, needing her in a way he hadn't needed a woman in a long time.

He didn't know what it was about Kate that got to him, but her hold on him was fierce and powerful. When she'd asked him to kiss her, he'd felt like she'd yanked his feet out from under him, leaving him struggling for balance. He hadn't bothered with women in a long time, not since he'd found his fiancée naked with the guy who had one more zero in his net worth than Cole did.

Her infidelity hadn't surprised him, and he hadn't really cared one way or the other. He'd gotten the ring back, tossed it in his dresser, and gone back to the office. He simply hadn't cared about her, or anything, enough to have it bother him. But Kate was different. He barely knew her, but every inch of his soul was already craving her. He felt like fire was burning through his veins, searing every cell in his body.

"Cole," she whispered his name as she wrapped her arms around his neck, pulling him more tightly against her.

Cole. The way she said his name made something turn over inside him, something that yearned for more. His entire being was responding to her, desperate for her, needing more than a kiss, needing more than one minute in a driving storm. With a low growl, he deepened the kiss. It quickly turned fiery when their tongues met, unabashed and needy—

The boat pitched, knocking them both off balance. Cole swore and grabbed the edge of the container, barely keeping them upright. She clutched his arm, her brown eyes searching his.

Those eyes. Shit. He *knew* them.

"It's snowing," she said, her voice filled with awe as she looked up.

Cole didn't bother to check out the sky. Instead, he

watched the tiny snowflakes dotting her dark hair, settling on her shoulders. It was snowing hard already, the flakes whipping horizontally from the wind. He didn't want to look up. He just wanted to look at her.

The ferry dropped suddenly, and she yelped, grabbing his arm as they both slid across the now-damp deck. Even his boots weren't going to be able to hold once the deck got saturated, not in this kind of storm. "We have to go inside."

She met his gaze, searching his face, as if she were waiting for something else from him.

"What?" he asked. He knew she wanted something from him, but he had no idea what it was.

Disappointment flashed across her face, as if he'd somehow let her down. "Nothing," she said with a shrug he didn't believe. "I just don't want to go in."

"I don't either." Once they went inside, the moment would be over. He'd be besieged by people he'd once known, people who would treat him like the person he'd once been. He'd be swept away from Kate, this kiss, and the intimacy they'd found on this deck. He wanted to be here, outside, with Kate, where nothing he was or had ever done mattered. He wanted to know what it was she'd wanted from him, that he hadn't given her.

For a long moment, they stared at each other, fighting for balance in the rising storm. He wanted to stay on the deck with her forever. He wanted to kiss her again and again, until he ferreted out her secrets, or got her out of his system. Either one would work. Going inside now left too much unfinished... which was maybe a good thing.

He wasn't here for a woman, and he wasn't here to get involved.

He was here to cut the last tie to his past, and then never look back. Kate Smith, whoever she was, was not part of that.

It was time to go inside, for the last time, so that he could finally leave it all behind forever.

But he didn't want to go.

He wanted to hold onto this moment forever.

But he already knew that moments like this one didn't last. It was over before it had even begun.

* * *

Willow dragged her suitcases over the threshold of the Stone House Cottage, the bed and breakfast she'd made reservations at two weeks ago, when she'd made her desperate decision to run away from her life for Christmas. She was shivering from her short walk from her rental car to the front door. The rear wheel drive vehicle had barely made it up the snow-coated hill to the Stone House, and she was tired, cold, and yes, a little cranky about the fact that Cole hadn't remembered her.

Yes, they'd been fifteen, and it had been one magical kiss in the moonlight years ago, but still. She'd remembered that kiss. That was why she'd come back. Not for Cole, but because that night with him was the only night she'd really felt alive in her life, and she was terrified that her heart was turning to stone with each passing day.

The kiss with Cole on the ferry had been magical, but she'd been almost relieved when he'd been swept away by the local folks once they went into the lounge, welcoming him back as if he were a long lost hero. She didn't want to get involved with him, or anyone. It was too risky. She just wanted to find her spirit again, by herself, with just the joy of strangers helping, strangers who knew nothing about her and had no interest in trying to ferret out all her secrets for the world to see.

"Welcome to Stone House Cottage, and Merry Christmas!" A cheerful woman with gray hair in a bun, a bright red holiday sweater, and blue jeans walked down the hallway, wiping her hands on an apron decorated with Christmas ornaments and holly. She beamed at Willow, her twinkling blue eyes making Willow want to smile back. "Let me help you with your bags!"

The woman hurried over and grabbed one of Willow's suitcases, dragging it into the foyer. Willow followed her inside, then paused, staring in awe at the lobby of the inn. A huge Christmas tree took up an entire corner, decorated with shiny ornaments and real candles. Christmas lights were strung across the walls, Santas were placed on every table, and there were even bright red stockings hung by a beautiful stone chimney. Christmas music was playing in the background, and the most delicious scents of fresh bread and pumpkin pie were wafting in from the kitchen. "It's beautiful," she breathed, all the tension fading from her body. It had been the right decision to come to the island. This was exactly what she'd wanted.

The woman smiled. "We do Christmas right on Mystic Island," she said. "Some of our guests have been coming here for three generations, because there's no place that does Christmas the way we do." She set the suitcase down and held out her hand. "My name's Rosie Wilson. You must be Elizabeth Jespersen, right?"

Willow shook her hand, grinning widely. Rosie's enthusiasm was contagious, a welcome change from Cole's rejection of the island's magic "No, I'm Will—"

She cut herself off. "I mean I'm Kate Smith."

Rosie's brows knit. "Kate Smith?" she repeated. "Is the reservation under your name? Because I don't recall that name. Elizabeth Jespersen is the only one who hasn't checked in yet."

Sudden foreboding pressed at Willow. "I just made it two weeks ago."

"Two weeks ago?" Rosie's brows knitted even further. "We've been fully booked since last January. You couldn't have made it two weeks ago..." Suddenly her face cleared. "Oh! You booked for next Christmas, right?"

"What?" Willow's stomach dropped. "Next Christmas? No, this Christmas. Today."

Rosie walked over to the front desk and began typing on the computer. "No, see? Right there." She turned the monitor so Willow could see it. Sure enough, beside her name was a reservation for exactly one year away.

"Oh." Willow's heart sank. "I didn't mean for next year. I meant this year. There has been a misunderstanding. Do you have anything? I don't need anything fancy."

Rosie clucked gently, giving Willow a look of sympathy. "I'm so sorry, sweetheart, but we're completely booked, with a full waiting list. Everyone in town is at maximum occupancy. We always are at this time of year."

"You mean...there's nowhere to stay? At all?" As she said it, she heard the blast of the ferry horn as it headed back to the mainland, no doubt hurrying to beat the storm. "Surely there must be something available somewhere in town? I mean, I can't leave, right?"

"No, you can't." Rosie sighed, rubbing her chin.

"The only thing I can think of is that the Ocean Heights Inn might have space. It's been closed for the last six months, and they weren't planning on being open this season, but the owner is back in town now, so maybe you could barter a room for yourself."

"Really?" Hope leapt through Willow. "Do you have their number?"

"Sure." Rosie picked up a rotary phone and dialed. She listened, then hung up. "The answering machine is still on, and it's full, so clearly the messages haven't been checked. You'll have to go over and talk your way in."

"Okay, great. No problem." She was desperate. Surely in a town like this, they wouldn't turn her away, right? Someone would let her bunk down *somewhere.* "Which way is it?"

"It's at the north end of the island," Rosie said. She eyed Willow skeptically. "Do you have a good car?"

"Um..." She tried to remember what kind of rental she had. "It has rear wheel drive."

"Well, if you don't have at least front wheel drive, you'll never make it there if you wait much longer with the snow coming down the way it is." Rosie walked around the table and picked up Willow's bag, giving her a thoughtful look. "You know, I don't think it's a fluke that you came here with-out reservations and nowhere to stay."

Willow wearily picked up her bag and followed Rosie back outdoors into the biting wind. She shivered when the wind hit her, whipping the breath right out of her lungs. "Why is that?"

"The island chooses people. If it called you here, it had a reason. If you had waited to get a reservation, you would never have come, because you couldn't have gotten one." Rosie opened Kate's rear door and tossed the heavy bag in as if it weighed nothing.

Willow's heart skipped. "You think it's chosen me?" She remembered Cole's story about the island's legend. She'd come here to find herself again. Was she destined to find it?

Rosie eyed her. "Maybe. Either that, or you just bought yourself a long week of sleeping in the back of that car and living off canned beans. You'll know soon enough."

Willow blinked. "Canned beans?" Surely Rosie was kidding. "I'll find a place to stay, even if the Ocean Heights Inn won't take me."

Rosie slammed the car door shut. "No, you won't. There's not a spare bed in town. It's your only option." She grimaced. "And I'll be honest, sweetheart, I don't think it's a very good one. Let's hope the island has a plan for you, because you're going to need some help."

4

*H*E DIDN'T WANT to be here.

Not for a single minute.

Cole stood grimly in the front hall of the house he'd grown up in. The old building that had once been full of warmth, people, and history now stood stark and empty, with a coating of dust on everything. He remembered each piece of furniture, and even the paintings were exactly the same as when he'd left. It was as if time had stood still inside the house, without even a whisper of change...except that it was now eerily empty.

The only sound was the ticking of the grandfather clock in the living room, the clock he'd been responsible for winding once a week. How was it still going?

Hell, he didn't want to be here for a minute, let alone a week.

Grimly, he set his bags down. They hit the hardwood floors with a thud. He remembered polishing those floors with a wax his dad had made from goat's milk and honey from their own backyard. Now, they were dusty and dull, so far from the standard his dad would ever have allowed.

He took a deep breath at the thought of his father. There was nothing he could do now. He was gone, and this was Cole's legacy to dispose of.

The windows rattled from the wind as Cole walked further into the house, flipping on lights as he went. Most of the light bulbs were still working, casting a sleepy glow into the shadows, and over the couches that someone had covered with sheets to keep them clean. It looked like a mausoleum, and felt like one, too. This wasn't his home anymore. It was just an empty building that meant nothing.

His job this week was to get it in shape to put on the market, to turn it into something a stranger would want. Hell, he'd give the damn thing away if he had to. He just wanted out—

A knock sounded at the door, and he grimaced. His brief stop in the grocery store for enough supplies to last the storm had put him over the edge. Too many questions about where he'd been and why he was back. Too many people who wanted to talk about his mom's funeral six months ago. He wasn't interested in socializing. His plan was to stay low profile, clean up the house, and then get out. He didn't even know what to say to people anymore. He'd grown up here, but now he felt like a stranger.

Ignoring the person at the door, he continued to head back toward the kitchen, when his visitor knocked again. "Hello? Is anyone there?"

He jerked to a stop and spun around, adrenaline

racing through him. He recognized that voice. Kate Smith was at his door.

Despite his best intentions to be antisocial, he couldn't help the surge of anticipation. Kissing her had rocked him on his heels, and he was intrigued by her. She wasn't a threat to his need to stay disconnected from the island, because she had nothing to do with the past he was trying to leave behind, or the present that he wasn't all that enthralled with either. She brought her own sphere of existence, and that was exactly what he was in the mood for.

She knocked again, louder this time, and he heard her muttering under her breath about the cold. He couldn't help the grin that spread over his face as he strode toward the door. He pulled it open, just as she started to knock again, resulting in a fist to his chest. He caught her hand in his, grinning at her startled expression.

"Oh, sorry." She jumped back, her eyes widening when she saw him. "Cole? *You* live here?"

"Yeah." He frowned at her obvious surprise. She hadn't tracked him down on purpose?

"Is this the Ocean Heights Inn?"

She was asking about the inn? He narrowed his eyes. "Yes, it is." She couldn't have a reservation, because they'd all been cancelled. The day he'd buried his mother, he'd had his admin cancel all the reservations, even the ones who'd been coming for decades. They could take a year off. He'd felt a little guilty at shutting down the inn, but he'd decided it would be good for them to learn that this coastal Maine island wasn't all that the world had to offer. "It's not open for business, though."

"Yes, I heard." She lifted her chin resolutely.

"There was a mistake in my reservations at the Stone Cottage. I don't have a room, and the ferry doesn't come back for a week. I need a bed. I don't care if it's clean or fancy, I just need a place to sleep."

His eyebrows went up, and anticipation rolled through him. "You want to stay at my inn for the *week*?"

"Yes. I'm desperate. Please? I'll pay whatever you want. I...I have money."

The slight hesitation in her last sentence made him realize that she hadn't wanted to admit she had money. Whoever she was, she was hiding from something, or someone, from a life she wanted to escape during the season when most people sought out their loved ones.

He knew about walking away from his life. He was here to sell the inn, but he was also here because he hadn't wanted to spend Christmas in New York City, going to all the parties he'd been shortlisted for. He studied her more closely, noticing the desperation in her eyes, the lines of stress around her mouth. Something inside him softened, something that hadn't been soft in a very long time. He didn't want to be with others this Christmas, but Kate was different. She made him want to care, and it had been a long time since he'd cared about anything.

He wanted her to stay.

Slowly, he stepped back and held the door open for her. "It's not in shape for guests, but if you can handle dust and cobwebs, you can have your pick of the rooms."

Her face lit up. "Really? Oh, wow, you're the best!" She gave him an impulsive, genuine hug, making him feel like more of a good guy than he'd felt in a very long time...and it felt good.

Damn good.

* * *

Willow swallowed with sudden nervousness as Cole stepped back, gesturing for her to come inside his inn. Being wrapped up in his arms on the ferry deck had been a moment of reckless abandon and intimacy in a winter storm, a moment of connection that had no future. On the ferry, he was a shadowy figure who'd provided warmth and security. Now, he was simply a man. His coat was off, revealing a navy blue fleece that was unzipped to reveal the collar of a light blue oxford. His jeans were dark, in perfect condition, but they hugged his lean hips with the intimacy of a woman. There was a faint hint of whisker stubble along his jaw, and his eyes were dark brown, studying her so intently she felt as if he were peering right into her soul.

He was pure male, and she was walking into his territory, inviting herself into his lair. On the ferry, it had been neutral territory, a fantasy buffeted by the storm and the waves. Walking into his inn to stay there was so different. Intimate. Being with him was no longer simply an elusive snapshot in time. It was reality, a moment that would stretch into a night, and a morning, and days. How long could she hide who she was under that kind of scrutiny and closeness?

She glanced at her car, suddenly wishing she could jump in and drive back to the life she'd been so quick to run away from, but her rental was already covered in a sheet of snow. Plus, she doubted it would handle all that well across the stretch of Atlantic Ocean that separated Mystic Island from the mainland.

"I'll get your bags," he said, his voice rolling

through her. "Come inside. You're shivering."

"It's okay." She turned toward her car, eager for an excuse not to take that step into his house. "I can get my stuff—"

"I'm on it." He slipped past her, his shoulder brushing against hers before he vaulted down the slippery steps with ease. He reached her car in a few easy strides, paused for a moment to flip her windshield wipers up so they weren't touching the glass, then grabbed her luggage, and strode back inside. He raised his eyes at her as he passed, holding the door open with his foot to keep it from swinging shut. "You coming inside, or what?"

"Yes, of course." She peered past him into the foyer. "Is there anyone else here?"

He grinned, a mischievous smile that made her heart skip. He was handsome when he was being serious, but his smile took her breath away. "No. Just me. Why? Are you afraid?"

She lifted her chin, giving him a haughty look. "Of course not. Why would I be afraid of you?"

"Because you already know what a great kisser I am." His smile faded. "I have to be honest with you, Kate. Kissing you was incredible. If you stay here, you need to know that it's going to be on my mind."

Heat flushed her cheeks. "Are you saying I'm not safe with you?"

"No. You're safe. I'd never do anything to make you uncomfortable." His gaze dropped to her mouth, and then back up. "But I'm not a saint. I'm not going to be able to forget that kiss."

Her heart began to race. "You think you won't forget a kiss with me?"

"I know I won't."

"Don't make promises you can't keep." When his eyebrows went up, she realized she might have pushed it a little far. It wasn't as if she wanted him to remember what had happened between them so long ago, because if he remembered, then things would change. She didn't want them to change. She wanted to be anonymous.

"I never do." He leaned back against the door, holding it open with his body. "You still want to stay here? Just you and me, and a great kiss that neither of us is going to forget any time soon."

A part of her wished that the inn was busy so there was a buffer between her and Cole, with his mesmerizing kisses and his intense stare. Despite his warning, she felt completely safe with him. He'd kept her safe many years ago, and he'd been her protector on the ferry. She trusted him in a way she didn't trust anyone else in her life, and that was a great gift. Her whole body began to relax as the reality of her situation settled on her. Since no one else was at the inn, she didn't have to worry about pretenses, or being identified. Cole clearly didn't recognize her, so she could just drop all façades, venture out into town when she wanted to, and retreat back to the inn when she needed to escape.

Willow grinned, her first genuine smile in what felt like a very long time. "I am thrilled to stay here, actually. I think it will be perfect." She beamed at him, and then stepped across the threshold into the entry.

Her smile faded almost immediately when she saw what she had walked into.

The Ocean Heights Inn was magnificent from the outside, a classic New England charmer perched on a bluff that overlooked the ocean. A wide clearing stretched behind it, and she could imagine lawn chairs lined up while guests enjoyed a gorgeous summer day playing croquet or badminton before heading down toward the beach. She loved the isolation of it, away from the bustle of the crowds. There was something so magical about it...until she walked inside.

It was covered in dust, furniture was shrouded in sheets, and it looked like no one had lived there in years. It smelled musty and old. In contrast to Rosie's Christmas coziness, this was just...depressing. "Wow."

He shut the door behind her. "It used to look great," he said. "When my dad was alive, this inn was the preeminent holiday lodging on the island. My mom kept it going pretty well until she died earlier this year."

"Oh..." Immediately, she felt guilty about noticing the lack of holiday decoration. She remembered when his father had died so long ago. That had been what had drawn them together that night. She'd forgotten about it. She'd forgotten so much about that night, but it was coming back to her slowly. "I'm sorry."

He glanced over at her as he strode down the hall, flicking on overhead lights as he went. He gave her a small smile. "Thanks."

Just one word. No explanation. No emotion...and yet, there was so much weight in his voice and in that brief flicker of a smile. She hurried to catch up as he vaulted up the stairs, still turning on lights as he went. "I haven't been upstairs yet," he said. "I don't know what shape it's in."

"It's no problem. I'm sure it's fine. Do you have any Christmas decorations in boxes? I could help set up." She strode after him, pausing halfway up the stairs to look at a photograph on the wall that caught her eye.

She caught her breath, staring at the image of the boy she'd kissed so long ago. "That's you," she whispered, brushing her finger over the dusty glass to clear it. There he was, the exact image of the boy she'd held in her memories all these years. She even remembered the bright yellow swim trunks, and the white beaded necklace he'd been wearing. His dark brown hair was tousled, too long for fashion, but perfect for a boy who lived on an island. He was laughing, his eyes crinkled up with such amusement that she smiled, her heart warming. "This picture was from that summer, wasn't it? I remember that swimsuit—" She caught herself, biting her lip before she could say anymore.

When Cole didn't say anything, she looked up. He was on the top of the landing, staring down at her with a shocked look on his face. Electricity seemed to leap through the air, and she froze.

He remembered.

5

*I*T WAS *HER.*

Cole's gut thudded in disbelief as he stared down at her. How could he not have recognized her? He could see the girl from the beach in every line of her face. He recognized the vibrancy of her brown eyes, the tilt of her nose, the way the left side of her mouth tilted up a tiny bit higher than the right when she smiled. Her voice brushed over his skin the way it had before, a little throaty, and decadently sensual. It was *her*, but he was sure her name hadn't been Kate back then.

Her cheeks turned pink. "You remember me."

It wasn't a question. It was a statement, and he knew then that she remembered him. Her luggage slipped from his hand, landing with a dusty thud on the landing. "Willow."

She smiled then, a smile that seemed to light up her face. "Hi."

"Shit." He vaulted down the stairs and landed beside her, searching her face. A thousand questions raced through his mind. Where had she gone? What was her last name? What life did she lead? But he didn't ask them. He simply touched her cheek, just as he had that day so long ago when they'd run into each other on the beach. She'd been in tears from something her mother had done, and he'd been agonized by the death of his father. Two teenagers, hopelessly outmatched by life, had found hope and solace in each other on a sandy beach in the moonlight. "You look the same," he said softly.

Her smiled widened. "Which is why you didn't remember me until now?"

"I didn't know. I wasn't looking for you." He picked up a lock of her hair. So soft. It was darker now. Back then it had been a lighter brown, streaked with blond, but it was a deep chestnut now, rich and sexy as hell. "Did you come here for me?"

She shook her head. "I didn't know it was you until after the kiss. I just never forgot how this island made me feel, and I wanted to come back. I didn't come for you, just for how you made me feel." Her cheeks turned even pinker. "I wanted to spend Christmas here. That was all. Once I realized it was you, I wasn't going to say anything. But then I didn't have a room, and I didn't know this was your place. I wasn't stalking you, I promise—"

He smiled then, a goofy grin that made him feel like an awkward teenager all over again. "If I'd known it was you on the ferry, I would have made you stay here with me." His fingers slipped through her hair. He still couldn't believe she was there, standing in front of him. He'd almost believed she'd been a figment of his imagination. "I looked for you the next day, but you were gone."

She nodded. "Summer ferries run every day. We were gone on the eight o'clock boat."

"I would have gotten your number." He searched her face, drinking in all that he hadn't had the chance to so long ago. "I would have called you. Tracked you down. But I didn't know how to find you, and your family had left no contact info at the inn. Just gone. No one at the inn had ever heard of a girl named Willow staying there, though you fit a description of someone named...Jane? Is that what it was?"

She shrugged. "I could have been registered under Jane. We used a lot of different names over the years."

He tugged lightly at her hair, still shocked by the fact she was standing in front of him. "What's your real name? Willow or Kate? Or Jane? Or something else?"

She hesitated then. He felt it in the sharp intake of her breath, and he saw it in the way her gaze flicked away from his for a split second. His fingers tightened in her hair, as if he were a teenage boy again, desperate to hold onto the one thing that seemed to make sense. "I need your real name," he said, his voice hoarser than he'd intended. "Tell me who you really are."

Her gaze flicked back to his. "Willow," she said softly. "I gave you my real name the first time. You're the only one I told the truth to when we were here before. I wanted you to know the real me."

His grip softened in her hair, and a sense of rightness flooded him. She looked so vulnerable staring up at him, her face cast in a golden glow from the dusty sconces on the wall. She was no longer a teenager, hiding from her parents in the darkness. She was a woman, but her eyes were the same, full of the same vulnerability as before, still hiding behind a façade, just as she'd done so long ago.

But, he was no longer who he had once been, a teenage boy overwhelmed by his terror about death and loss. He was a man now, a man with money and power, a man who was in a position to help and protect...and this woman, this magical moonlight goddess from his past, mattered to him, because she'd saved him from such darkness so long ago. "What are you hiding from?" he asked softly. "What's chasing you? How can I help you?"

Longing flashed across her face, but she shook her head. "I'm here to leave it behind," she said. "Can you let me do that?"

It. She'd said *it.* Not *him.* Not another man who had a claim on her. Relief rushed through him, and he nodded, willing to give her time...because they had a week. A week until the ferry could spring either of them. A week with the woman who'd changed his life so long ago.

She smiled, a smile that made his heart glow with a light that hadn't burned in a very long time. "Thanks."

He grinned back. "The beach is kind of cold and snowy right now. How about I get a fire started and figure out some food and drink, and we pretend we're fifteen again?"

Her smile widened. "I'd like that."

"All right, then." He searched her face. "When we were fifteen, I kissed you."

Her smile faded. "You also kissed me twelve years later."

"You think I should wait another twelve years for the third kiss?" He knew he was pushing her comfort zone, but he didn't care. The need to taste her again was almost insurmountable. She wasn't simply the woman on the ferry who had called to him. She was *Willow*, the woman who had been a part of his soul for more than a decade. She was unfinished business, a story whose ending had never been written, and he'd waited too long for the chance to finish his dance with her. He wanted that moment to start right now.

Her gaze flicked to his mouth, and then back to his eyes. He saw the yearning in them, and he knew she felt the same connection between them he did. She was drawn to him, but she was always wary, fearful, and protective of herself, because he'd pushed her too far.

Shit. He wasn't going to be that guy, the one who made her uncomfortable. He dropped his hand from her hair and forced himself to step back before she could answer. He'd seen her cry before, and there was no way in hell he was going do anything that could bring her more pain, no matter how much he wanted to kiss her. "Sorry. Too much. I'm the innkeeper, and you need to feel safe here." He didn't miss the relief in her eyes...or the regret. "I'll show you to your room, and then meet you downstairs when you're ready. It'll take me a little bit to locate the firewood and get things going, so take your time. Sound good?"

She nodded. "Yes, sounds great."

"Okay." He started to turn away, then froze when she put her hand on his arm.

"Cole?"

He turned back toward her, his entire soul burning from the feel of her hand on his arm. "Yes?"

"Thank you." She stood on her tiptoes and pressed a kiss to his mouth, the same tender, sweet kiss of so long ago. Her lips tasted of sea salt and wind, just as they had on the ferry. He cupped her face lightly, and kissed her back, resisting the urge to turn the kiss into the heated fire that was pouring through him.

The kiss was too short, barely started when she pulled back, her gaze searching his. "You don't know who I am, do you? My last name?"

He frowned. "Should I? Did you tell me?"

"No. I just..." She smiled again. "I'm glad to be here."

He brushed his finger along her cheek. "Yeah, me too." And as he said it, he realized it was true. He'd avoided the island for over a decade, and he'd done his best to delay this visit for as long as possible, but now that he was here, with Willow, he couldn't think of any place he'd rather be.

Yes, she was hiding secrets.

Yes, it was only a week, and then they both had to go back to their lives.

And yes, neither of them were innocent teenagers anymore, and there was no way to ignore the heat smoldering between them, heat that was too dangerous to play with...but he didn't really care.

Sitting in front of a fireplace with Willow was going to lead to things. He knew it. Getting entangled with her wasn't what he'd come here for. It wasn't something he had space for in his life, not for a day, or a week, or longer.

But he didn't care.

He was going to build that fire, and when she came downstairs...yeah, well...he wasn't going to let her get away so easily this time.

He wanted at least one last dance before their story ended.

* * *

An hour later, Willow paused in the doorway to the

living room, her breath catching when she saw Cole standing in front of the hearth, watching the flames blazing in the fireplace. The flames cast flickering light and shadows across his face, accentuating the strong line of his jaw, and the bronze highlights in his dark hair. His arms were folded across his chest, and his expression was moody and troubled, utterly exposed and vulnerable. She had a feeling she was seeing a side of Cole that not many people got to see, because he kept it hidden so carefully.

His jeans and heavy winter boots were covered in snow, giving him the look of a true Mainer. He'd changed his shirt, and he was now wearing a cashmere crewneck sweater that looked incredibly soft and expensive, but the collar of his shirt was peeking out, revealing an old tee shirt beneath his expensive sweater. He was a mix 'n' match, fitting in wherever he went...or maybe nowhere at all.

He looked over suddenly, and smiled, the moodiness chased away by a warm smile that made her heart skip. "Hey."

She smiled, feeling a little shy. "Hi."

He picked up two glasses of wine from the mantle, one red and one white. "I didn't know which you wanted, seeing as how you weren't a big drinker last time we met."

"Red would be great." She took a deep breath and walked into the living room. The sheet had been tossed off the couch, but the room was still dusty and kind of dreary. She could smell something cooking that made her stomach rumble. "You're cooking?"

"It's an inn. It's what we do. Not a lot of menu choices tonight, though." His fingers brushed hers as she took the glass, and her heart skipped. "It's been a while since I've been in that kitchen, so it's possible I might have made some egregious substitution, like salt instead of sugar or something like that."

"That's fine. I'm sure it's delicious." She stood awkwardly in front of the fire, facing him, not sure what to say. Now that their past had been identified, where did they go? It wasn't as if they'd had an extensive relationship back then. Just a day, one amazing day. "So, um...what do you do for work?"

His eyes narrowed. "Really? That's your question?"

She blinked. "What?"

"That's not how it was before."

She stiffened. "Cole, we were fifteen, and it was one day. There isn't really a before—"

"Before, we didn't talk about trite, meaningless things. You told me how you felt like your heart was shriveling inside your body because you belonged nowhere in this world, and you felt like you would never be good enough. I told you how my father had just died, and my mom was already dating someone. I told you how I hated having to be at this inn every night when my friends were out playing. I told you that I didn't want to be in the inn anymore, because it just reminded me of my dad and how my life would never be again. That's what we talked about, not what schools we went to or what music we liked."

She stared at him in shock. "You remember all that?" The moment he'd said it, the memories had come tumbling back. She knew he was right. The connection between them had been instant and profound, not littered with the superficial interactions of awkward teenagers.

He reached out, sliding his hand through her hair. "What are you running from, Willow? What made you decide to celebrate Christmas by yourself on an island in Maine? What's trying to break you this time?"

His voice was so gentle, and so familiar that tears suddenly filled her eyes. Maybe he was why she'd come. Maybe she needed him the way she'd needed him before—a stranger who cared, but was so distant from her real life that it was safe to let her guard down and be honest with him, and with herself. "I just wanted to know what it would be like for Christmas to matter."

He searched her face, his fingers still tangled in her hair. "What do you mean?"

"For my whole life, we've been on the move. Christmas was just like any other day. My parents were always working on different projects, so we were never together. Christmas was about parties and being seen by the right people. I've never had a Christmas tree. I've never woken up to stockings hanging from a mantle or had Christmas dinner with people who cared. I just...I just wanted that, and I remembered you telling me that Mystic Island had the most special Christmases in the world...so I wanted to come. I wanted to feel what Christmas is really like." It sounded so lame she was embarrassed, but it was the truth.

He put his hand over her heart, his palm warm. "You think Christmas will fix what's broken in here?"

She bit her lip and shrugged, somehow not surprised that he'd realized that her yearning for a real Christmas was driven by a deeper hole in her heart, one she didn't know how to fix. "Maybe it will start a chain reaction of some sort."

He laughed then, a deep, masculine laugh that made her smile. "A Christmas chain reaction. That's something my dad would have said." His smile faded as he spoke, and his gaze drifted to the wall behind her.

She turned and saw he was looking at an old oil painting of an attractive young couple. The man looked a lot like Cole, maybe a little younger than he was now. "Your parents?"

"Yes. They had it painted the year they bought the inn. I thought the red and green Christmas sweaters looked ridiculous, but they loved Christmas and wanted the holiday spirit to last all year long in this place." His voice was softer than it had been on the ferry, as if some of his hard edges were slipping away.

"Why did you come back here?" she asked. "After so many years away?"

He glanced at her. "My mom died over the summer. This was the first chance I've had to get the place cleaned up and ready to put on the market. Once I sell it, my ties to the island will be cut completely."

Her heart sank at his words. "You really don't want to be a part of this place?" The magical place that was supposed to save her was his hell?

He said nothing for a long moment, just staring at the painting. Finally, without looking at her, he said, "The good that was once a part of this island is long gone for me now. There's nothing here for me except..." He paused, his gaze flickering to hers. "Except pain."

"Your father dying?"

"And more. Other stuff. His death was only the beginning."

"Of what?"

He hesitated. "Of—" A buzzer sounded from the kitchen, and relief flashed across his face. "Dinner. Wait here. I'll bring it out." He set his wine glass on the mantle and slipped past her, not inviting her to join him.

Willow sighed and turned to face the fireplace, her fingers loosely wrapped around the stem of her glass. There was still a chill in the air, the kind of chill that happened in a house that no one had been living in for a while, from heat that hadn't been used in too long. What else had happened to Cole? When they'd been on the ferry, he'd mentioned losing someone in a storm. Her throat tightened at the idea of him facing more loss. Wasn't his father dying enough?

She blinked back sudden tears and took a deep breath. She'd come here for Christmas spirit, not to trap herself in a past of loneliness and grief. Did she really want to go to dark places with Cole?

She didn't even know what she wanted anymore. All she knew was that when he'd come vaulting down those stairs to touch her cheek, it had felt like that was the moment she'd been searching for her whole life.

"Here." Cole strode out of the kitchen, a red, fuzzy Santa cap on his head, and another in his hand. "My mom and dad used to go crazy with holiday decorations. I found these, so it'll have to suffice for the moment." He set it on her head, and tugged it straight, his face completely deadpan. "There. Much better."

She laughed at his serious expression. "This is your Christmas celebration? Santa hats."

"It's the start. I'll find the rest of the stuff tomorrow." He stepped back, eyeing her hat like a designer evaluating his art. "You want Christmas, and this is the place to be. I'm on it." He turned to head back to the kitchen. "I'll be back in a minute with the food."

"Cole?" She reached out, catching his arm.

He paused, setting his hand over hers so she couldn't pull away. "What?"

Her heart ached at the feel of his hand on hers. God, she'd forgotten how special he made her feel. She'd forgotten what it felt like to be so comfortable with him, to feel like she mattered. "You don't have to create Christmas for me," she said. "I know you're not here to be an innkeeper. Just let me crash here, and I'll go into town for my holiday spirit. It's okay, Cole. You don't have to fix my world."

He stared at her for a long moment, as if contemplating her words. Then he lifted her hand off his arm, and brought it to his lips. She caught her breath as he pressed a light kiss to each knuckle. "I know I don't have to," he said. "I want to."

Then he released her hand and walked out.

6

COLE COULDN'T EXPLAIN precisely what it was about Willow that awakened such a powerful need to help her. Maybe it was because she'd been the only one who'd seen him cry when his dad had died, not that he'd intended to bawl in front of a girl, but she'd stumbled across his hiding place when the shit had become too much for him to handle.

Maybe it was because he was the one who'd held her while she'd cried on his shoulder so long ago. And maybe it was because he needed to do something that was actually worthwhile.

His dad had believed in Christmas. He'd believed that the holiday could restore life to the dying, health to the sick, and love to those who no longer believed. Since his death, Christmas had never been the same. It had become a poor imitation of a holiday that had once mattered. Ever since, Christmas had been just a bitter reminder of what Cole had lost, and he'd hated the holiday.

But when Cole had stood in front of his dad's goofy Christmas portrait with Willow, discussing how she wanted Christmas to matter, something had shifted for him. By giving Willow the Christmas his dad believed in, maybe Cole could honor his dad's legacy one final time before selling the inn. A Christmas chain reaction, words his dad would have loved, that defined what he'd believed Christmas should mean.

Cole might not believe in Christmas anymore, but he once had, and he knew how to present it in a way that would touch anyone's heart. It was what he had ingrained in him from the first moment he was born. He didn't have to buy into Christmas to give Willow one that would matter to her. That was one thing he could do for her, even if she wouldn't talk about what she was really running from.

So, first on the agenda was food. Good food made a difference. Whistling softly, Cole pulled the roasted chicken out of the oven and plated it with the panache his mom would have approved of. He was actually kind of impressed with the display when he finally had the potatoes and asparagus salad dished up. Some skills apparently didn't fade despite a decade of rust and a lifetime of resistance.

He paused long enough to grab an advent candle out of the pantry, tucking it under his arm while he snagged utensils and their dinner. He could almost hear his dad ordering him to deliver it with a smile as he walked out of the kitchen, and he felt himself grinning as he walked down the hall toward the living room. It had been a very long time since he'd tried to make someone's Christmas better, and he almost felt like he was a kid again, trying to live up to his dad's legendary legacy.

When he stepped inside the living room, Willow was seated on the couch, her arm draped over the back and her feet tucked under her. Her hair had been damp from the shower when she'd walked in, but it was beginning to dry, cascading over her shoulder in loose waves, just like it had so long ago after they'd gone for an evening swim. She looked exactly the same as she had as a teen...but at the same time, she was a thousand times more beautiful. The tiny lines around her eyes gave her depth, the curve of her hips made her a real woman, and her eyes carried a lifetime of wisdom in them. "Hey."

She looked up, and a warm smile lit up her face. "It's so surreal to see you standing there," she said. "It's like it was only yesterday that we were on that beach."

"I know." He grinned as he hooked his toe around the leg of the coffee table and dragged it over to the couch. "It's cool."

Her smile widened. "Cool?"

"Yeah. Cool." He set the plates down, arranging them on either side of the candle. He retrieved his wine and the matches off the mantle, and within moments, he had a decent ambiance established. The whole time he was setting up, she was watching him silently, her big, brown eyes following him until he finally sat down beside her on the couch. He raised his glass. "To a Christmas chain reaction, and innocent teenagers."

She smiled and lightly touched her glass to his. "To kisses that waited for twelve years."

He met her gaze, and they both went still for a moment. The air between them seemed to sizzle with electricity, and a raw need pulsed through him. "If you keep talking about kisses," he said in a low voice, "I'm going to have trouble remembering that you're a guest at my inn."

"Sorry." But she didn't sound sorry, and her voice was rough, almost breathless. "It's just..."

"It's just what?"

She met his gaze. "I can't think of anything I want more than for you to kiss me again. I know it's silly, but I can't help it. I missed you. I missed how you make me feel."

His fingers tightened around his wineglass. "When we were fifteen, kissing you rocked my world. But I'm not fifteen. It's not going to stop at kissing this time, and we both know it."

She swallowed. "You feel it, too?"

"Feel what? Like we left something unfinished twelve years ago? I can't even think around you because your pull on me is so strong." He set his wineglass down and leaned in toward her, letting his fingers drift across her collarbone. "I look at you, and I want to be the one to start that chain reaction for you. I want to be that guy. I know how to make Christmas special, and you make me want to do it for you. You make me care and I haven't cared about much besides work in a very long time."

Her eyes widened, but she didn't pull back. "How can I feel that way, too? We don't even know each other."

"Maybe we don't know the superficial stuff about each other," he concurred, sliding his hand across her cheek. "But we bared our souls to each other, and that's so much more. I've seen your heart, Willow, and I want to heal it."

Tears filled her eyes, and she wrapped her fingers around his wrist. "Cole—"

"No words. Not right now." He closed the distance between them and kissed her, their third kiss, one that had all the sensuality of the one on the ferry, and the connection of the one so long ago. He couldn't keep the kiss light. The moment his lips touched hers, the kiss turned molten, a seduction ignited by the white-hot fire roaring through him.

Her grip on his wrist tightened, and she leaned into the kiss, welcoming him. It was different from the one on the ferry. That had been intense and fiery, ignited by the storm. This one was a kiss between people who had a connection that had been held in tenuous memory for too long.

This time, she tasted of wine, sensuality, and innocence. He slid his hand through her hair and deepened the kiss, unable to resist her allure. She palmed his chest, her fingers digging into his sweater, as if she couldn't decide whether to push him away or pull him closer.

It didn't matter. If she pushed him away, he'd find a way to stop himself, but right now, he liked having her hand on him. Heat began to rise between them, and he pulled her closer, until her breasts were brushing against his chest. She leaned into him, one hand sliding down to his hip, where she slipped her fingers into the belt loop of his jeans, tugging lightly.

Need pulsed through him, the kind of need he hadn't felt in a long time. He wanted more, he needed more, he—

Her stomach rumbled, and she burst out laughing in the middle of the kiss. "I'm so sorry. I'm just really hungry."

He grinned, pausing to steal one final kiss before finally releasing her. He hadn't eaten in hours either, not that he would have stopped kissing her to eat. "I'm a great chef. Your stomach is smart to demand food instead of sex."

"Sex?" She raised an eyebrow at him as she picked up her fork. "Maybe it would have just been a kiss."

He gave her a skeptical look that made her chuckle again. He realized he loved her laugh. There was something incredibly magical about it. Irreverent and light. Contagious. It made him want to laugh, and it had been a long time since he'd wanted to laugh. "Yeah," he said. "I'm sure it would have just been a kiss."

A complete lie, and they both knew it.

* * *

Willow bolted awake to a loud clanging that jerked her from her sleep. She sprang upright, and almost fell off the end of the couch onto the floor. She had a split second to remember that she was in Maine, on a couch with Cole, when he grabbed her and hauled her back onto the couch, tucking her against his side. "S'okay," he muttered sleepily, his eyes still closed as he wrapped his arm around her. "Just the storm."

His arm was strong and reassuring, and the heat from his body was pure temptation, so she sank back against him instinctively, her body relaxing into him even before she'd woken up enough to process exactly where she was. Her body melting into him, Willow looked around, trying to regain her bearings and figure out exactly how she'd awakened in Cole's arms.

The fire was out in the hearth, leaving behind nothing but gray embers. The living room was freezing, and the lights were low. The windowpanes were rattling fiercely, and the wind was howling, making her realize it was the storm that had dragged her from her dreams. The night was dark outside, the kind of deep darkness of the middle of the night in a place where there were no streetlights or fluorescent signs.

Their dinner dishes sat on the coffee table, along with their empty wineglasses. She smiled when she remembered the delicious dinner he'd served, and how much fun it had been to talk to him, both of them trying to recall more details about their night together so long ago. Her comfort with him was as automatic as it had been when they were younger. Her cheeks heated up as she recalled getting sleepy after dinner, and how she'd leaned into him, lulled by the sensation of peace. She realized that she must have fallen asleep in the middle of their conversation, and he'd apparently decided to stay with her instead of waking her up. Contentment warmed her, and she lightly tapped his arm. "Cole?"

He mumbled something and turned on his side, draping his leg over her hip and tugging her more tightly against him. The position put her intimately against him, with her belly pressed up against the front of his jeans...which made it clear that he was having some sort of interesting dream. Awareness leapt through her, the kind of delicious, sensual awareness that made heat pulse low in her belly. His thigh was solid muscle, weighing her down, and his body was strong and warm, protecting her against the chill in the air. His breath was warm against the side of her neck, and she closed her eyes, unable to resist the allure of being in his arms. She felt utterly safe with him, so far away from her life, and the pressures and judgments she lived with every day. Cole knew nothing of who she was supposed to be. He'd seen only her true self, the side that wasn't hopelessly trapped by expectation and superficiality.

She sighed and ran her hand along his arm where it was locked around her waist. The hair on his forearm was soft, and his muscles were defined and toned, the body of a man born to survive a physical life on a rocky Maine island. What would it have been like to grow up here? Where everyone knew her name, and no one wanted anything from her? Where there could have been more stolen nights on a beach with Cole?

"You okay?" His voice was more alert now, and she turned her head to see that he was watching her. His eyes were dark, half-closed, but they still bore into her with the same intensity as before, as if he were trying to see into the very depths of her soul.

She liked how he looked at her, as if he didn't care about the outside, only the inside, which she didn't show to anyone.

She rolled over to face him, tucking her hands under her chin so they were lying face-to-face, only inches apart. It was too close for strangers, but their proximity felt natural and right, even though she barely knew him. With his leg over her hip, his arm around her waist, and their bodies pressed against each other, there was no hope of any kind of proper distance between them...and she didn't want to move away. Being close to him made her feel like she could breathe for the first time in a very long time. "Why did you leave here?" she asked. "Wasn't it amazing to grow up knowing everyone, and feeling like you belonged?"

He lifted one shoulder in a casual shrug. "Once my dad died, it was different. My mom got remarried in less than six months to the owner of the hardware store. Most people said they were already in love before my dad died, and I didn't like hearing that much. He had three boys, and family holidays changed. They outnumbered us, and their traditions won. My mom even started closing the inn for Christmas so we could hang with her new family. It wasn't my world anymore."

She heard the coolness in his voice, but she wasn't fooled. She'd feigned the same indifference too many times when talking about her own family, and her heart softened for him. Maybe in some ways, they weren't that different. He could talk about it like it meant nothing, but to a child, home meant everything. "I never had a real home growing up," she admitted, snuggling more tightly against him to ward off the cold. "If I had, and then I'd lost it, I think I would have been devastated. Losing something is harder than never having it, I think."

He studied her, his eyes dark. "What's your last name?"

She hesitated. She didn't want her real life to come into the moment, but at the same time, a part of her wanted Cole to see all of her. Maybe, he would see something about her that she didn't. "Morgan," she said softly. "My name is Willow Morgan." She held her breath, waiting for that moment of recognition, but he just repeated the name softly.

"Willow Morgan," he said, his deep voice making her shiver. "That's a beautiful name. Why didn't you want to tell me?"

She hesitated. "You don't recognize my name?" Her name had been dragged across the tabloids so many times during her life. Her baby pictures had been sold to a gossip magazine for over a million dollars. Her awkward teenage years had been ridiculed on social media. Her first attempt at acting had been brutalized online. Everything she'd done in her life that should have been private had been made public, strewn across people's phone and tablet screens to judge and talk about. How could Cole not have stumbled across something about her, and her A-list parents?

He picked up a lock of her hair and rubbed his thumb across the strands. "Should I?"

"Well, I mean...I guess not." She could tell he wasn't lying. Her name sparked no recognition for him. Slowly, the most wonderful sense of freedom began to sweep through her. Cole had no preconceived ideas about who she was, or who she should be. To him, she was simply the girl he'd met so long ago, and the woman he'd found on the deck of the ferry. How was that possible? "Don't you read the newspapers? Or magazines?"

He shook his head, his gaze settled thoughtfully on her face. "I read business publications. Other than that, I live under a rock." His eyebrows went up. "Why? Are you famous? Should I be intimidated by you?"

She laughed at his irreverent tone, all the tension draining from her body. She didn't know how he had no idea who she was, but it was such a relief, a gift. She'd hinted enough about her life, and he didn't care about it. "Yes, you should. I'm terribly scary."

His low laugh echoed through the cold room. "Sweetheart, I don't really care if you're the first princess of Britain. To me, you're the girl who saw me cry and gave me my first kiss."

Her heart skipped a beat at his endearment. "There's no such thing as a first princess of Britain," she said. "And how was that your first kiss? You were totally hot. What boy hasn't had his first kiss by then?"

"A boy who had no interest in girls until he met a certain girl in jean shorts and a red tee shirt." His eyebrow cocked and he leaned closer, so close she could feel the warmth of his breath on her lips "Why do you ask? Wasn't that your first kiss, too? It had to be."

She lifted her chin, suddenly feeling hot. "Why were you so sure it was my first kiss? Because I was so bad at it?"

"No." His eyes softened. "Because it was so beautifully innocent and pure. I always figured I was your first. I wasn't?"

Heat suffused her cheeks. "You were," she admitted.

The corner of his mouth lifted ever so slightly. "I knew it."

Silence grew between them, and her heart started to race. She was so conscious of every place their bodies were touching, the intimate way their legs were tangled, the feel of his fingers still stroking her hair, the heat of his body against her belly. When they were fifteen, the intimacy between them had been innocent. Now, it was completely different, intimacy layered with a deep awareness of Cole as a man, and herself as a woman.

"What about sex?" he asked, his voice low and rough. "Have you been waiting for me to be your first there, too?"

"Seriously?" She slapped his chest, laughing despite the sexual tension wrapping so tightly around them. "What kind of question is that?"

He caught her hand and pressed a kiss to her palm. "Like I said earlier, sweetheart, I'm not a fifteen-year-old boy anymore who isn't interested in girls. I'm a man, and—" He stopped, cutting himself off.

She pressed her lips together, her heart sinking. What had he been about to say? Some cocky, arrogant remark about sex? "You love women? Is that what you were going to say? You love sex?" Her warmth faded, and her emotional defenses sprang back into place with effortless efficiency. "You like to sleep around?"

"No." He caught her wrist as she tried to pull back. "I don't sleep around. I've slept with one woman in the last five years. I dated her for three years, and we got engaged. When she decided to sleep with a friend of mine, I cut her loose, didn't give a shit, and didn't bother with women again. I don't have baggage. I just don't care enough to make it worth my while."

She swallowed at the edge in his voice. She didn't even know which of his statements to respond to first. "Your fiancée cheated on you?"

"Yeah." He slipped his hand behind the back of her head, tangling his fingers in her hair. "When I stood there in the doorway, watching the two of them trying to get their clothes back on in a hurry, I felt nothing. I realized that I hadn't expected anything better from her. I wasn't surprised, and I didn't care."

She searched his face, and saw that he was telling the truth. "How could you not care? When my fiancé—" She stopped as the old pain welled up. Dammit. She didn't want to revisit that part of her life. It wasn't worth all the energy it had already sucked from her, let alone any more. She didn't want that to be a part of this moment with Cole.

"You were engaged?" He frowned. "Not anymore? What happened?"

She shrugged. "It's not a big deal. It doesn't matter—"

He tugged on her hair, drawing her attention to

him. The moment she looked at him, he kissed her softly, so tenderly, so gently that she wanted to cry. His lips were a whisper across hers, gone before they'd even been there, a kiss every bit as perfect as that first one he'd given her so long ago when he'd kissed away her tears back then. "My sweet Willow," he said. "Tell me. I want to know."

God, how could she tell him what had happened? He'd realize what a mess her life was.

She shook her head, tracing her finger along his jaw. The whiskers prickled her fingertips, whiskers he hadn't had when she'd known him before. "Cole—"

He caught her chin with his hand, and lifted her face to his. Her breath caught, and she realized he was going to kiss her again, one that was more than a whisper across her lips. He searched her gaze, and time seemed to freeze between them. Her fingers tightened instinctively on his jaw, and then he smiled, a small, quick smile before he moved in and kissed her.

7

*H*IS MOUTH TASTED of sin and passion, and the kiss was pure heat. Her fingers curled in the front of his sweater, tugging him closer as she kissed him back, unable to resist the allure of his seduction. No, not seduction. Something more pure and elemental than that, a connection that ran from her soul to his, a mingling of breath, laughter, and pain. It was a kiss of intimacy and private connection, a kiss to remind her who she was with, a kiss that made her feel like she was the only person in the world that mattered in that moment. He paused the kiss, their lips still touching, and her breath caught in anticipation, a heartbeat in time, both of them waiting to see what direction it would take.

After a moment, he pulled back just enough so she could see his face. One hand was in her hair, stroking it back from her face as he studied her. "It was bad?" he asked. "Your situation with your fiancé?"

She smiled. "You kissed me to drag the story out of

me?"

He shrugged. "Seemed like a good excuse to do what I wanted to anyway." He cocked an eyebrow. "So, talk to me. That's what we do, remember? We pour the shit out to each other and take away its power. Tell me what happened."

She sighed, and leaned her head against his shoulder, resting her cheek against the softness of his sweater. "You thought it was bad when your mom shacked up with the hardware store owner and his boys?" He didn't smile. He simply waited. With a sigh, she ran her finger over his chest, drawing designs on the finely woven fabric. "Well, I was engaged to the first man who had truly won my heart, until my mother called me into her office and told me that *she* was going to marry him instead." Ugh. Just saying the words made her feel like such an idiot. How had she not seen it coming? How had she been such an idiot?

Cole's eyebrows shot up, and she felt heat suffuse her cheeks as he stared at her. "Really?"

"Really. They got married a month later." She averted her gaze away from him, fixating on a hairline crack in the ceiling, remembering all the questions and the looks. The whispers. She'd had no time to grieve in private. Instead, she'd been forced into a public display of nonchalance. "I was the maid of honor at their wedding. It was the only way I could get people to stop talking. I had to make everyone think I didn't care." That had been the hardest thing she'd ever done in her life, to stand there and pretend she was above it all. "I don't trust easily, and I believed in him. I trusted him... and..." She blinked back tears that she'd thought she was past as Cole continued to stroke her hair. "I don't know which betrayal was worse, my mom or him. In a way, he was worse, because I had long ago stopped counting on my mother, but still—"

"Hey." Cole touched her chin, drawing her attention back to him. "People can suck," he said softly. "It's not your fault. They suck, not you. You were right to be upset. It's bullshit that they treated you like that."

She looked at him then. "How could I have been so wrong? I never trust, but I trusted him. I just...I don't want to live like that anymore. I don't want to be a part of a world where people have agendas that are more important than being good people. That's why I wanted to come here. I wanted just one week, one holiday, one Christmas, surrounded by people who wouldn't do things like that to the people they claim to love, you know?" She put her hand on his chest, over his heart. "You had the same thing happen with your fiancée, but I can tell it didn't bother you. You're hard, Cole. I don't want to be hard. I want to be able to love, but I don't think I can do it anymore. I'm scared, I'm bitter, and I don't believe." She searched his face. "I need to believe again, Cole, and I'm terrified that I never will. I need magic to touch my heart again, or I'm afraid it will shrivel up and die."

He framed her face, his touch incredibly gentle. "You have too much heart for it to ever stop loving," he said. "I can feel the beauty of your heart, and I don't feel much anymore. You're right that I'm hard now, and I like it that way. It's a better way to live...but when I'm with you..." He leaned closer, his breath warm against her mouth. "When I'm with you, I want to be the guy I was when I was fifteen...I want to make you smile again, and I want to feel what I felt that night with you."

And then he kissed her again...not a sweet, tender

kiss, but a deep, intense kiss that sent fire searing through her body. She knew instantly that this wasn't a kiss that would stop. This was a kiss that had no ending, one that would explode into flames that would incinerate every last defensive barrier locked around her heart. It was lust, passion, and desire, a kiss that would never let her go...and her heart burned for it. Instinctively, she gripped the front of his sweater, holding on tight as she melted into him.

The moment she kissed him back, the kiss turned molten. He growled low in his throat, and tightened his leg around her hip, dragging her so tightly against him that there wasn't room for even a sliver of air between them. His fingers tunneled through her hair, making her want to nestle even more tightly against him. She loved the feel of his hard body against hers. She loved his hands in her hair. He tasted incredible, and his kiss took her breath away.

His hand went to her butt, drawing her hips against him, and she felt his erection against the junction of her thighs, through their jeans. Apprehension rippled through her, and she froze, a thousand emotions rushing through her. Desire. Need. Fear. Want.

He immediately went still, pausing in the middle of his kiss. For a split second, neither of them moved, and then he pulled back, releasing her hair. "Sorry."

Cold air whipped across her as he pulled back, leaving her bereft. "It's okay—"

"No, it's not." He extricated himself from her, leapt to his feet, and stood there, his hands flexing by his sides. His hair was tousled from her hands, and his shirt was untucked. With his whiskers and hooded gaze, he looked dangerously sexy, a man born for sin and seduction. "You just told me that you're afraid to trust. I had no right to put you in that position. Shit."

Her heart ached at his regret, and she sat up. "No, it's okay. I just panicked."

"I should never have put you in a situation that made you feel panic. *Shit.*" He ran his hands through his hair, and she saw the flash of a watch on his wrist, an obscenely expensive brand she'd seen on the wrist of many men over the years.

She stared at him in surprise. He was *wealthy*. She'd known he wasn't the local innkeeper or an island kid who lived on a beach anymore, but to see that watch made her realize exactly how far from that he was. He was a man with money and a life far away from here, a man who might not be so unlike those she was running away from.

He turned away, bracing his hands on the mantle as he bowed his head, taking a deep breath. Above him hung the picture of his father and mother in their adorable Christmas sweaters. Willow's gaze settled on that picture, and she saw the love in his parents' eyes, especially his father. There was so much warmth in his face, so much love in the way he held his wife's hand. They had loved each other, truly loved each other, and that was what Cole had grown up with.

He turned toward her. "I'll take you out to breakfast in the morning," he said, his voice so business-like and reserved that her heart sank. "I'm going to make this Christmas what you deserve. I'll give you the Christmas my dad would have given you. Tomorrow, there's a Christmas Eve holiday pageant and dance, and a snowman festival in the afternoon. We can build one if you want. I can hook you up with the carolers. They go out every night. We missed the Christmas tree lighting in the town square. That happens the day after Thanksgiving, but they flood the area and freeze it, so there's a skating rink. You skate?" He glanced at the window, though it was still dark outside. "If it has snowed enough, I'll take you snowmobiling. I'll just have to check the gas and tune it up. It's the best method of transport after a snow." He turned away, muttering to himself. "The decorations must be around here some-where. We'll find a tree and put it up." He swore under his breath as he headed to the door. "Another Christ-mas in Mystic," he muttered. "Who'd have ever thought?"

"Cole." She scrambled over the back of the couch, almost falling on her face when her foot caught on the pillow. He caught her arm before she fell, holding her upright. His face was dark and moody. "You don't have to do this for me. Give me a Christmas, I mean."

"I want to." He stared down at her, his face a stoic mask. "My dad would shoot my ass from heaven if he knew I didn't take care of you. It's what he lived for." He started to turn away, but she caught his arm again, drawing him back. "What?" he snapped.

She didn't back off, knowing he would never hurt her, even though he was angry. "When you got off the couch instead of kissing me..." She paused, searching for the words that would make sense. "No one has ever done that for me. Walked away because they might hurt me. People in my life don't do that."

The tension in his jaw eased somewhat. "I won't be that bastard to you—"

"I know." Her heart ached for him. He had no idea who she was, other than the girl he'd met on the beach. Nothing he was doing was for ulterior motives. He was just real, and he was hers, for tonight. His heart had broken when his dad had died, and Christmas had died for him as well...and yet, he was ready to do whatever it took to give it to her. That, alone, made her feel like the most treasured person in the world. "Kiss me," she said softly.

His face become shuttered. "No."

"Why?" She moved closer to him.

He stiffened. "Because I want to."

She stopped in front of him, searching his tormented face. "I know we both have to go back to our lives in a week, but we have tonight, right? You've become so hard that you feel nothing...except I make you feel, don't I?"

He looked past her at the wall, his jaw flexing. "Yeah."

"And you make me feel like I can breathe again. Isn't that worth something? To each other? To us? Don't we both deserve what we give each other?" She reached out and took his hand, surprised at how cold it was. "Cole?"

He finally tore his gaze off the wall and looked at her. "I don't want to simply kiss you," he said, his voice raw and hoarse. "I want to make love to you a dozen times before dawn, and never get out of bed the rest of the day. I want to learn every inch of your body, I want to know every secret in your heart, and I want to heal them all. I want to come alive with you, and hold nothing back. If I kiss you, I'm not taking you anywhere on the snowmobile today. If I kiss you, I'm going to take you to bed, and I'm not going to stop making love to you until I have nothing left to give you." His eyes darkened with smoldering heat. "If I kiss you, you're mine in every way, until we get back on the ferry."

Warmth pooled in her belly, and she smiled. "I

know."

"Do you?" His hand snaked out and locked around her back, forcing her against him. He searched her face. "I want all of you, Willow. And you have to take me. No halfway. No holding back. No secrets. I hate superficial crap, and that's not what I want with you."

She nodded. "Okay."

"Okay?" He looked incredulous. "That's all you have to say? Okay?"

"I'm nervous. I'm excited. A part of me has been hopelessly in love with you since that night when we were fifteen, and the other part of me, the grown up part of me, has fallen right back in love with you, in that instantaneous, electric way that has nothing to do with logic, and everything to do with survival, so yes, okay. Kiss me, and don't break any of the promises you just made to me."

He swore under his breath, and slid his hand through her hair. *"Willow."* He whispered her name a split second before his lips captured hers in a kiss that was every bit as electric as that one so long ago...but this time...it wasn't an innocent exploration. It was pure, sizzling heat, ignited by the gaping emptiness that they both lived with, the emptiness that disappeared only when they were together.

"Cole." She whispered his name into the kiss as she wrapped her arms around his neck, melting into his strong body as she kissed him back. The kiss turned ravenous, a frenzied assault of passion, lust, and need that tore through her shields and right to her heart. She needed more of him. More skin, more closeness, more of everything. "Your sweater." She tugged at the offending garment, and he yanked it and his tee shirt over his head, tossing them aside, his heated gaze never leaving her face.

His body was lean and muscled, taut with strength, but she barely had time to appreciate it before he was kissing her again, backing her across the room as he tugged her shirt out of her jeans. His hands were searing hot on her waist as he palmed her sides, sliding his hands up her ribs as he swept her shirt upward. His thumbs grazed her nipples through her bra, and then her shirt was off. He tossed it aside, and then the couch hit the back of her knees.

He caught her as she lost her balance, taking them both down to the narrow couch. The kiss was frantic now, as if twelve years of pent-up need had been released in a raw, uncontrollable frenzy. He cupped her breast as he kissed her, sliding his fingers beneath the lace to caress her nipple, a tantalizing tease that made her squirm with need. Her entire body felt like it was burning up. Need coursed through her stronger than she'd ever felt, need for him, for them, for everything.

She reached between them, trying to find the fly to his jeans, but the minute she touched his zipper, he rolled off her, yanking his pants off with record speed, his eyes burning into her. He was gloriously muscled, pure male, so primal and wild, a man who belonged on this rugged island, far beyond the boy she'd once known.

"You're more beautiful than I ever could have dreamed," he said, his eyes sweeping over her half-naked body. "A treasure. *My* treasure."

Tears burned in her eyes at the reverence in his voice. He meant it. This tormented, kind, handsome man thought she was truly beautiful. "Thank you."

He grinned, a wicked gleam in his eyes, then he kissed her again, taking over the couch as he stripped off the remainder of her clothes.

Then, suddenly, finally, there were no barriers between them. His body was searing hot against hers, his kisses stripping her of all coherent thought. He sat up and dragged her onto his lap so her knees were on either side of his hips. He kissed her with desperate need, his hands tunneling through her hair. His erection was against her belly, hot and hard, and her breasts were crushed against his chest.

He swore and broke the kiss, his hands still buried in her hair. He pulled back enough to see her, his eyes dark with the same need that burned through her. "This matters to me," he said softly. "So little matters to me anymore, but this does."

She nodded, her breath tight in her chest. "Me, too."

"My dear, sweet Willow." His strong hands clamped on her hips, and he lifted her up, his gaze never leaving hers. "Mine." He lowered her gently, easing her down as his erection slid inside her damp folds.

She gasped at the rush of sensation, at the desire that flooded every part of her. "It's never been like this," she said. "It's never been you."

"I know, sweetheart. I know." He dragged her against him, burying himself in the kiss as he moved his hips, driving inside her. He didn't let her go, assaulting all her senses on every level, turning the kiss and the lovemaking into a fierce unleashing of passion.

She gripped his shoulders, moving her hips, taking him more and more deeply inside her, moving with and against his rhythm, until there was nothing left but the fierce connection between them, spiraling heat twisting tighter and tighter as the orgasm built. He moved his hips again, shifting his angle, and she was lost to him. The orgasm exploded through her, and she gasped, her entire body clenching as it took her. His arms locked around her, holding her up as he followed her over the precipice, his body jerking against her as he was swept up in the heat between them.

When it was finally over, Willow sagged against him, too exhausted to hold herself up, resting her face in the crook of his neck. She'd never felt so thoroughly loved, or so thoroughly sated in her life. "I don't want to move," she whispered.

Cole kissed her forehead, a deep laugh rumbling through his chest. "You don't have to, sweetheart. I've got you."

She sighed and relaxed into him, breathing in the scent of him. *I've got you.* Three words that no one had ever said to her before...except once, many years ago, beneath a full moon on a beautiful beach, by a boy she'd just met. Words she'd forgotten, until now. Words she never wanted to forget again.

8

$\mathcal{H}$E WOULD NEVER get tired of her smile.

Cole grinned at Willow, watching the wonder on her face as she took in the Christmas lights lining the street. There were wreaths hanging from every telephone pole, and twinkling white lights glittered under the snow on every bush. The powder was soft beneath their boots, muffling the sound the way only a fresh snow could do. With the soft snow still thick on the trees and roofs, and the Mystic Island decorations, even he could feel the Christmas magic humming in the air...or maybe it was just the magic that Willow brought with her wherever she went.

They'd spent the rest of the night and most of the day in bed. He'd learned every inch of her body, what she liked, what she loved, and how she loved it. She was vibrant in bed, igniting a fire in him that had been dead for a long time. He loved her playfulness, and her spark, and each time, his smile felt more natural and less foreign. She'd given him her body, and a reason to care, and now he was going to give her the Christmas she'd been searching for.

Cole tugged Willow's hand, coaxing his reluctant date along the stone pathway that led to the island's community center. "Come on, slowpoke. You won't want to miss this."

"I think maybe I do. Can't we just walk down to the dock? It's so beautiful tonight. Who needs people?" She looked adorable in one of his old stocking caps they'd found when they raided his closet, looking for clothes that would keep her warm. It was blue and white, the colors of the Mystic Island high school, and it made her look like she was his high school girlfriend, not the woman he'd spent the last eighteen hours in bed with. Her cheeks were flushed red from the cold, and her nose was pink. "We could get takeout and go back home," she suggested hopefully, her gaze flicking nervously to the people streaming past them into the charming brick building.

"Never. This is Christmas Eve on Mystic Island, babe. It involves people, not just snow. You can't stay home and miss it." He threw his arm around her shoulders, tugging her close as he steered her toward the double doors that were propped open. It had been years since he'd been to the Christmas Eve pageant and dance at the community center, and he was surprised that he was excited to see it. "I was in this when I was a kid. I used to be a great singer. I got the whole town rocking. You should see me do my Elvis impersonation."

"You were a good Elvis?" She cocked her eyebrows at him as they walked up the stairs. "Really?"

"I'd never lie about that." He hesitated for a split

second when he saw familiar faces begin to turn toward him, and fingers pointing his way. Shit. Was he really going to do this again? He'd been so intent on bringing Christmas to Willow that he hadn't thought about facing his old 'hood, the people he'd left so long ago. He looked down at Willow, and saw her peering past the crowd into the chapel, her eyes widening at the sight of all the Christmas decorations, and his doubt faded. For her, he could do this.

"Cole?" A hand came down on his shoulder, and he turned. He recognized the weathered face in an instant. It was one of his best friends from high school, Luc Pelletier. His hair was darker, his shoulders wider, and his eyes more weighty, but it was him. "You really back?"

"Hey, man." Cole couldn't help but grin, and he thudded Luc on the back when his friend pulled him in for a hug. Damn, it was good to see him. "You look great. What's going on? Did you and Janice ever get married?"

His friend's eyebrows went up in surprise. "Yeah, and she took off when our boy was a year old. Never heard from her since. I've been doing the single dad thing for almost eight years. You didn't know?"

Cole grimaced. "Sorry, man. I had no idea." He noticed then the weariness in Luc's gaze, the kind of weight that could bring even the strongest man down. "You should've called."

"Didn't have your number, but it's cool. We're good. Being a dad is the greatest gift ever." Luc grinned then, that same bold grin he'd always had. "But glad to have you back, buddy. This island's too quiet without you. You opening up shop again? Heard you already got the rooms filling back up."

Cole cleared his throat. "Actually, no, I'm selling the place."

Luc stared at him, his gaze burning into him. "What? Why?"

Cole was surprised to find that Luc could still get to him the way that only someone who had known you most of your life could. "Because it's not my place anymore."

"Fuck that. It's been waiting for you all these years. You can't sell it. You gotta run it."

Cole suddenly felt tired, the same kind of tired he felt every time he thought of the island. "It's complicated."

"Fuck complicated. You just make it complicated, just like you always did." Luc suddenly turned to Willow, who had stepped slightly off to the side, out of the conversation. "Luc Pelletier," he said, extending his hand. "You Cole's woman? If so, you need to snap his head on straight. He belongs here, and he knows it. He's just too damn scared to stand up and face it. He's been running for over a decade, and it's time for him to stop."

Willow's eyes widened, but she shook Luc's hand. "My name's...Kate Smith," she said. Her gaze slated toward Cole. "Cole's okay," she said, looking back at Luc. "He knows what he needs to do, but I'm sorry about your wife."

Luc's face softened. "Appreciate it, Kate. It's been a while, but you never forget, right?"

She nodded, then she smiled back, a genuine smile that lit up her face. "Right."

The two of them smiled at each other, and suddenly a wave of jealousy shot through Cole. He narrowed his eyes, and took Willow's hand, gently tugging her closer to him. "So, we'll see you inside then?"

"Yeah, you got it. Watch for the third sheep. That's my boy." Luc winked. "He was so mad he was a sheep. It's highly uncool. I told him you were a sheep for six years in a row, and he felt better."

Cole laughed then, the tension easing from his body. There was nothing like being around people who knew he'd been a sheep for more than half a decade. "I was a damned good sheep."

"That's why you never got out of that role. If you're too good at being a sheep, you never get to be a king." Luc nodded at Willow. "Maybe a dance later, Kate? I can tell you all of Cole's secrets, before he became a rich bastard with no time for the little people."

She grinned. "I'd like that."

Luc blew her a kiss, and she was still laughing as Cole took her hand. "He seems nice."

"Yeah, he's a good guy." Cole couldn't help but smile at the glow on her face. "He didn't seem to recognize you," he remarked casually. "Guess I'm not the only one who lives under a rock."

Her smile widened. "I noticed that too. Maybe I can just be me. Wouldn't that be great?"

"You should always be you." Cole tucked her up under his arm, and this time, when one of his old friends called his name, he didn't shy away. It actually, in a way, felt good to be back.

Maybe it had been right to come back and do a proper farewell to the life he used to have. His flight to Australia left the day after the next ferry landed on the mainland. He wouldn't be back to the States for at least three years once he got on that plane. This was his last moment, and suddenly, as he looked around at the faces he'd once known so well, he wanted to make it count.

He looked down at Willow, who was scanning the room with rapt attention, completely immersed in the moment, clearly not thinking anymore about being recognized. Something shifted inside him. It was Willow who'd gotten him out here tonight. Willow, who had made him think about Christmas again. Willow, who had made him start to care again. Willow, who'd gotten through to him when nothing else had.

She looked up at him. When she saw him watching her, she broke into a wide smile. "Thanks for bringing me here, Cole." She stood on her tiptoes and pressed a kiss to his mouth, right there in front of everyone.

Claiming him.

He immediately snaked his arm around her back and pulled her close, kissing her back, just to make sure that everyone knew he agreed with her claim.

* * *

By the time the last call for eggnog rolled around, Willow's cheeks hurt from laughing so much. She'd danced with just about every male in Mystic, including a six-week-old baby and the ninety-three-year-old man who ran the town gardens. Everyone was lovely, everyone was nice, and no one was perfect. She'd seen a man propose. She'd helped a young woman clean up her makeup in the bathroom after sobbing over her boyfriend who'd just dumped her. She'd fended off the town's animal advocate who was fostering three dogs and had tried to get Willow to adopt two of them. There were the wealthy people who'd retired to the island after years of summering, and there were those who were the lifeblood of the island, the fourth generation plumber, and the third-generation electrician, who knew everyone who'd been born on the island for the last hundred years.

People were too loud, too quiet, too friendly, and too merry, and she loved every minute of it because everyone was real. There were no pretenses, just people being who they were, for better or for worse.... including Cole, who was an incredible dancer, and clearly well loved by his town. He'd never left her side, making her feel like the belle of the ball. Even when he'd deigned to let Luc steal a dance with her, his eyes had never left her the entire time they were apart, making her feel like he was counting the seconds until she would be in his arms again. She knew she was, and he'd made it clear she wasn't the only one who felt that way.

It was, most definitely, a night she would never, ever forget, and for all the right reasons.

"The last dance is mine," Cole announced, sweeping in to grab her hand just as Luc reached for it. "Sorry, buddy, but you need to find one of your own."

He gave Luc an affectionate thud on the shoulder, then he pulled her out onto the dance floor as the local band launched into one of her favorite Christmas songs, one that had made her decide that grandmas and reindeers should never mix.

She laughed as he spun her around, moving with grace and fluidity that made her feel like she was flying. "I've had so much fun tonight," she said. "Is it always like this on the island?"

"Nope. We're real and flawed, but everyone's got your back, even if they're pissed at you." He grinned at her. "It's good to see you smile."

She laughed. "You too, even if you are a rich bastard who has forgotten the little people, according to

Luc and one of the women at the refreshment table," she teased, feeling so lighthearted. "I can't believe you want to leave this behind."

He shrugged. "It's not the same for me anymore," he said, shadows flickering behind his eyes.

Her gaiety faded somewhat. "I know," she said. "I've heard a lot about your dad tonight. He sounds like he was an amazing man."

Cole pulled her closer and nuzzled her neck. "He was."

She shivered, chills racing down her spine as his warm breath brushed over her bare skin. "And I met your stepdad. He's very nice."

Cole stiffened almost imperceptibly, and pulled back to look at her. "He's not my stepdad," he said curtly. "He married my mother. There's a difference."

She sighed, unable to forget the guilt, regret, and sadness in his stepdad's eyes. "He wants to talk to you. Why don't you give him another chance? He seems like he really loved your mother."

Cole's jaw flexed, and his gaze flashed to the corner, where his stepfather was standing, watching them. "Got nothing to say to him."

"Yes, you do."

Cole stopped dancing, his hands dropping from her waist. "Let it go, Willow."

She caught his arm before he could turn away. "No. You have so many people who love you, and you refuse to see it. Do you know what I'd do if I had this? I'd never let it go. I'd treasure every minute of it. Do you know how lucky you are?"

His eyes narrowed. "Willow, drop it—"

"Willow?" A teen girl passing by stopped suddenly, staring at Willow. "*Willow Morgan?*"

Willow's stomach dropped. *No, no, no.* Not here. Not now. Not when she was having such a good time. Not when she and Cole were talking about something so important.

Cole's gaze shot to the girl, and then back to Willow. He swore under his breath, then ensnared her wrist and pulled her into his arms, tucking her against him so his body provided a barrier between her and the girl. She buried her face in his neck, almost holding her breath as he swung her around the dance floor, toward the other end of the room. "I'm sorry, sweetheart. I fucked up by using your real name."

"It's not your fault. I don't want you to call me Kate." She needed him to see her for who she was, or the whole night was a lie.

"You okay?" His voice was low and reassuring as he spoke to her.

"Is she watching us?" She didn't dare lift her head.

"She's talking to other people and pointing at us." Cole's arm tightened around her lower back, and his fingers lightly grasped the back of her neck, tucking her more securely into the shield of his body. "What do you want to do? You want to leave?"

Dammit. No, she didn't want to leave. She wanted a night out like a regular person.

"Willow?" He spoke softly, too quietly for anyone else to hear. "What do you want to do? We can sneak out the side door. We're right next to it. I can take you down to the square to see the tree. It's amazing down there."

Was that really who she was? Skulking out side doors? Couldn't she be brave enough not to run away? She lifted her head to look around. Across the room, she saw two women pointing at her. Luc was beside them, his face shocked. She met his gaze, and she knew instantly that he no longer saw her as Kate Smith, a regular woman who he could tease and steal dances from when Cole wasn't looking. She was Willow Morgan to him, to all of them, and the night would no longer be the same. She didn't want her memories of the evening to be ruined. "Yes," she said quietly. "Let's leave."

"You got it. Wait here." Cole disappeared into the crowd, and then was back within moments, carrying their coats. "Let's go, sweetheart." He handed over her coat as he moved them stealthily toward the door, slipping her through the doorway so deftly it made her wonder how many times he'd snuck out the back door when he didn't want to socialize.

They shrugged on their jackets, but said nothing as he took her hand and led her through the snow around to the side of the old brick building. She kicked her borrowed boots through the snow, her footsteps silent in the powdery Christmas magic. She took a deep breath, trying to regain the mood that had felt so good before she'd been recognized, but it was elusive, chased away by the knowledge that people were talking about her now, repeating things that they'd read online, seeing her as fodder for gossip, not an actual woman.

Cole squeezed her hand. "We're here. Merry Christmas."

She looked up, and her breath caught when she saw the majestic Christmas tree. It was so tall, at least two stories high. It was covered with fresh snow, twinkling lights, and hundreds of ornaments. An angel was shining on the top, her white dress and wings almost blending into the new snow. It was majestic, breathtaking, and magical. "It's bigger than the one in Times Square in New York City," she whispered, unable to keep the awe out of her voice.

"Sure is. And it's a live tree. It's been growing there since long before I was born. Amazing, isn't it?"

"It's incredible." She walked up to it, unable to believe how huge it was. There were amazing glass ornaments that were works of art, and paper ones that looked like they were made by preschoolers, and everything in between.

"Everyone in town has at least one ornament that they've put on there. Anyone who is in Mystic for Christmas has to add one, so their visit will be immortalized forever." He reached into his pocket and held out a small box wrapped in gold tissue paper. "It's not much, but it's all I could come up with on such short notice. I couldn't break the tradition, though."

He'd brought her an ornament? "Oh, Cole. That's so sweet." Her heart softened as she took the package from him. "You didn't have to give me anything, Cole."

"Sure I did. Tradition." He was watching her closely, hopefully. "It's not much," he said again.

"It's everything." It didn't even matter what was in it. The fact that he'd brought her an ornament so she could hang it and leave her mark forever was so beautiful that it didn't matter what it was. She handed her mittens to him to hold, then carefully unwrapped the tissue. Inside was a small scallop shell with a piece of old brown string through a hole in the top. Her heart seemed to stop, and she looked up at him. "It's from that night, isn't it?" The night they'd met, she'd found a scallop shell on the beach, and she'd given it to him when they'd parted, telling him to keep it as a memento of the night. She hadn't really thought he'd keep it. She'd been teasing, trying to bring a little lightheartedness into a good-bye that had felt too heavy.

He nodded. "I wore it around my neck for a long time. I found it in my stuff today. Thought you should have it."

She brushed her fingers over the rough ridges. "You kept it all this time?"

"I hung it up on a nail inside my closet. It was still there when I looked this morning. My mom must not have seen it when she cleaned out my room after I left."

She tightened her finger around it. As much as she wanted to be part of the Mystic Island tradition, there was something about the scallop shell that made her want to hold onto it and never let it go. "It's beautiful." she whispered. "Thank you." She grabbed the front of his jacket and tugged him down to her so she could kiss him.

His lips were cold from the winter chill, but the kiss was instant heat and perfection, melting into the same passionate connection they'd shared since the beginning.

They were both grinning when he pulled back. "Go ahead and hang it," he urged, gesturing at the tree.

Reluctantly, she looped it around one of the branches and stepped back. The tiny white shell was almost invisible against the snow, and she felt her heart tighten. Was that what this time with Cole was going to be? Just fade away to invisibility? A part of her wanted to grab the shell off the tree, tuck her hand in Cole's, and race back to his inn to hold onto this moment with him.

He put his arm over her shoulder and kissed the top

of her head. "It's perfect."

"Won't it get lost? What happens if there's a storm and it blows away? Or when they take the ornaments off the tree? How will we know where it is next Christmas? What if we want to see it again?"

Cole raised his eyebrows at her in surprise. Then, without another word, he walked a few feet away from her, kicked the snow aside, and crouched down, feeling through the snow. He picked something up, twisted it, and then walked back over to her. "Hang this instead."

She looked down and saw he'd woven two broken sticks into a small wreath. "It's perfect." She looked at the shell from so long ago, and the wreath he'd just made. Suddenly, what had happened twelve years ago didn't feel as important as this moment with him. This moment was what she wanted to hold so tightly in her heart. "Can I keep the wreath instead?"

He smiled. "Anything you want."

"I'll keep the wreath." She folded it carefully in a tissue, and tucked it in the inside pocket of her jacket. "Should we go home?"

"In a sec." He wrapped his arms around her waist and pulled her against him, his dark eyes searching hers. "I need to know why there are so many shadows in your eyes. I need to know what made the holes in your heart. I want to know who you are, so I can chase away the darkness and fill it with light. Tell me your story, Willow Morgan. Who are you?"

9

COLE FELT WILLOW stiffen the moment he asked the question, but he didn't release her. He hadn't missed the look of absolute terror on her face when she'd been identified at the dance. She'd gone sheet white, and looked like a rabbit ready to bolt for cover. Whatever it was that had her spooked, he wanted to know what it was. "It won't change how I see you. To me you'll always just be the girl from the beach. Talk to me."

She searched his face, as if to ferret out any signs of subterfuge, and then she finally sighed. "You said you've been living under a rock, but surely you've heard of Billy Morgan and Ceci Ramirez?"

He frowned at her reference to two of Hollywood's biggest celebrities, superstars who'd had more than their share of scandals. They were infamous for affairs, on-the-set blowups, and Billy had been in and out of treatment for substance abuse over the years. They were both megastars, celebrities whose stardom had transcended the years and the scandals. "Of course."

She gave him a thin smile. "They're my parents."

"Your parents?" He frowned, trying to reconcile the ugliness of Hollywood celebrity life with the woman in his arms. "Really?"

"Really." She spread her hands. "I'm the ugly kid they hate to admit they have."

He narrowed his eyes, searching his memories for references to their children. "Isn't Angelica Morgan their daughter? And...a son, right? Trevor Morgan?"

"Yes, and me." She shrugged nonchalantly. "I'm the kid no one likes to acknowledge." She lifted her chin. "I'm the ugly, fat one," she said softly. "I never lived up to my family's successes. I'm just..." She shrugged. "Whatever."

He remembered suddenly seeing Ceci's wedding picture on the front of a magazine at a grocery store recently, and the groom who was twenty years younger. He hadn't paid any attention to it at the time, but as he looked into Willow's vulnerable face, he wished he had. *Hell.* "Tell me more," he said, sliding his hand into hers. "Let's walk."

She fell in beside him, her shoulder bumping against his as she began to fill him in about growing up in that family. The parties, the paparazzi, the constant judgment by the media. Her voice was tight and reserved as she spoke, but he could feel her pain anyway, especially when she talked about all her attempts to have an acting career like theirs, and how she'd always fallen short, never getting the role that would make her legitimate. "There was this one role I really wanted. It was for a fantastic movie. The director called my agent and told me that I was too fat and I needed a nose job if I ever wanted to get anywhere," she said softly. "I was sixteen at the time. It crushed me."

Cole swore under his breath, and pulled her to face him. "Listen to me, Willow," he said. "When you were sixteen, listening to some bastard say you were too fat, I was spending my Saturday afternoon at the dock, waiting for the ferry, hoping that the next one would bring you back to the island."

She frowned. "You were?"

"For the rest of that summer, and the summer after that, I met every single ferry that came to the island, looking for you. I watched every face that came off the boat, searching for you. I thought you'd come back, and I didn't want to miss it." He slid his finger under her jaw. "That's how amazing you were back then, and that's how amazing you are now. Every single ferry, sweetheart. I didn't miss a single one. I'd hear the horn, and I'd jump on my bike and haul ass down to the docks, no matter what I was doing." He still remembered his friends jeering him and his mom getting irritated, but that hadn't stopped him. He'd believed she would come back, and he'd wanted to be there for her the moment she stepped off the boat.

Turned out, he'd been right that she was coming back. Yeah, he'd been a decade early at first, but in the end, he'd still managed to be there the moment she returned.

Tears filled her eyes, and she gripped the front of his jacket. "I needed you back then," she said. "I needed someone to say that to me."

"You have me now," he said, bending his head to kiss her. Her lips were soft and sweet, tasting of eggnog and Christmas cookies, and heat instantly roared through him, the kind of heat that demanded nakedness, kisses that lasted forever, and orgasms that never let go.

Swearing, he broke the kiss, all too aware that if he didn't, he'd be pinning her up against the nearest building and doing things that would shock the inhabitants of Mystic Island. Instead, he caught her chin, letting her see the truth on his face. "And I'll say it as often as you need to hear it. Forget Hollywood, sweetheart. You're so much more than that superficial crap."

She smiled, a smile so beautiful and intimate that his heart seemed to stop and the night came to life. Unable to resist, he pulled her into his arms and kissed her the way he wanted to, with raw passion, desire, and a possessiveness that was so unfamiliar to him, but at the same time, so natural. As she melted against him, Cole knew that this was his moment. Nothing else in his life would complete him like kissing Willow by the docks on Christmas Eve.

Christmas might have died for him the day his father died, but tonight, for this one night, it lived on. Tomorrow was the first Christmas he'd looked forward to in a long, damned time.

But first...they had one more stop, one more thing he had to give her for Christmas, something she didn't even know she could have, something that only he could give her...with a little bit of help.

* * *

Willow hesitated as they approached the community center where the party was beginning to disperse, pausing when she realized that Cole intended for them to go back inside. The night had been so perfect with him, she didn't want to have to put up her emotional shields again, like she always had to in public. She wanted to stay soft, and she wanted to keep feeling the moment and her connection with him. "Let's skip it, Cole. I'd rather be alone with you."

But the stubborn man kept walking, his grip tightening on her hand when she tried to pull back. "I forgot my car keys," he said cheerfully. "It'll only take a second."

"What? That's a total lie." She narrowed her eyes at him, wondering what nefarious plan he'd hatched now. "Your keys are in your pocket. I saw you put them in there when we left."

He winked at her, keeping his grip tight around her hand. "I forgot my hat, then. Come on."

"Seriously? I don't need to go in there for that." Willow's heart began to hammer as he practically dragged her up the front steps of the building they'd just escaped from so surreptitiously. "Can't you respect what I want?"

"I am respecting what you want." He turned to face her, pausing on the steps. His eyes were soft with understanding, and he traced his fingers over her jaw, breaking through her tension. "Sweetheart, you wanted Christmas, right?"

She let herself lean into his touch, peace stealing over her just from the brush of his fingers. "Yes, but I don't need to go in there to have one. The present you gave me is everything I need. And…you." She hesitated before adding the last bit, unsure whether to voice it. Except it was true, and she wanted to say it. She wanted to feel her connection with him, and to acknowledge it.

He smiled, and leaned down to brush a kiss across her mouth. "Trust me. I have a present for you, but you have to come inside."

"Well…" She glanced past him, and saw people were already watching them with that knowing look she was used to, the one when strangers looked at her as if they knew all her sordid secrets. She sighed, feeling the same vulnerability creeping over her that she lived with all the time. "I don't want to deal with this tonight—"

He pulled her close then, his hands resting on her hips, his penetrating gaze searching hers. "Hey, babe, it's me. Don't you trust me?"

She stared into the dark eyes that had been a part of her for years. They were so familiar, and so comforting. Cole had been her source of strength for so long. Did she really trust him? He knew the reason she'd come to Mystic Island was to get away from her life. She searched his face, and knew that he would never put her in a situation that would take that away from her. "I trust you," she said quietly, the words both terrifying and exhilarating. The last time she'd trusted someone, she'd been betrayed. She was afraid to trust, but at the same time, she burned to have someone worth believing in again.

The pleased smile he gave her melted her heart. "Okay, then." He kissed her gently, then backed up, taking her hands in his. "Come in." He turned to walk into the party, his hand tight around hers.

Willow let out her breath, then allowed him to lead her into the room. He stepped inside the door, and she moved closer to him, wrapping both of her hands around his, as if somehow, he could be her shield.

The moment they stepped inside, Luc, Cole's childhood friend, headed right for them.

She stiffened, and raised her chin, preparing her haughtiest look, the one that kept everyone from pitying her. For a split second, she felt uncomfortable donning her shields, but it was so instinctual she couldn't help it.

Luc walked up. "You lied about your name. Why?" No preamble. No gawking. No treating her like a celebrity. He was challenging her, clearly irritated, and it almost made her want to smile.

No one ever treated her like a normal person. So, instead of deflecting his question with a socially neutral answer, she gave him the truth…not intentionally. It just slipped out, because Cole had already dragged her too far from her shell to make it easy to drive back in. "I just wanted to be me," she said quietly.

"You're not Kate Smith. You're Willow Morgan. If you want to be you, why the hell did you say you were Kate Smith?"

"Because…" She paused, realizing that in a way, his question made sense. "I don't want to be gawked at as the Willow Morgan people read about. I just wanted people to see me, as a person," she explained. She glanced at Cole and saw a small smile playing at the corner of his mouth. She realized suddenly that he'd done this on purpose. They hadn't come back in to get his hat or his keys. He'd brought her back in to face the crowds who knew her public persona, to keep her from running away from it.

Luc frowned, studying her thoughtfully.

"I didn't want to be judged," she added, trying to explain it better.

Luc grinned suddenly, and his face softened. "I get it, but you don't. It's not like that here."

She blinked. "Like what?"

"It's Mystic, Willow. It's not Hollywood. No one here has any time for the glitz and glam of anyone's life. Plenty of famous, wealthy people come here, and they come here because no one in Mystic cares about any of that shit." He glanced at Cole. "Just like it doesn't matter that he's some big shot now. He's just Cole, and he needs to open his damn inn again." His gaze landed on her. "Give it up, Willow Morgan. No one here cares who your parents are."

She lifted her chin, unwilling to surrender to the hope trying to surge through her. She didn't dare believe him, and then be caught unaware when she realized he was wrong. "They do care. I saw them pointing at me."

He raised his brows. "Yeah, okay, they do care, but not about some Hollywood crap. They care that your fiancé ditched you brutally. You need hugs, not gawking."

She sighed. "It's the same thing." The articles, the pity, the—

Cole nudged her. "No, sweetheart, it's not." He nodded across the room, and she saw Rosie, the woman whose inn she'd crashed, heading right for her.

Willow stiffened as Rosie approached, preparing herself... but the older woman said nothing. She just grabbed Willow around the shoulders and hugged her tightly. For a second, Willow didn't know what to do, then she saw Cole's grinning face. Slowly, awkwardly, Willow raised her arms and hugged her back.

Rosie's grip tightened, and suddenly Willow wanted to cry. Being able to lean on Cole had been special, but there was something about Rosie's hug that made her feel like she'd finally gotten the hug from her mother that she'd spent her life trying to win.

Rosie pulled back, her hands on her shoulders. "Listen to me, girl, and listen good. My no-good husband walked out on me when I had four kids under the age of six. If I didn't have this town to hold me together, I would have gone belly-up. I know it hurts now, but I'll tell you that you're the luckiest girl alive that you found out what he was like before you married him. Cry it out, then chalk it up as a narrow escape, and turn your eyes on the one who's worth it."

Her words were so genuine and heartfelt that tears filled Willow's eyes. "Thank you," she whispered, trying not to cry.

Rosie patted her shoulder. "Be proud that you found your own path. It's not easy to break away from your parents." She glared at Cole. "Of course, it's not always *right* to sever all your ties to your parents, but either way, it's never easy." Then she smiled at Willow again, a smile so full of warmth and love that it seemed to fill Willow's heart with light. "You bring Cole by for Christmas morning breakfast tomorrow. I doubt he remembers how to cook it the way it should be cooked." She winked at Willow, then turned away to corral a small boy who was trying to climb the Christmas tree at the far end of the room.

Willow stared after her in amazement, then became aware of Cole grinning down at her. "That's the way this place is," he said. "People are real. They care about who you are, not the superficial trappings. It's not just me. It's everyone in this place." He took her hand, and he pressed a kiss to her palm. "This place is your haven, Willow. Relax, and enjoy it."

She smiled, her heart filling up with joy. Cole was right. He'd given her the best Christmas present ever. "I'll relax on one condition," she teased.

His eyebrow quirked. "And what's that?"

"One more dance before we go?"

"You got it." He gave her wrist a tug, and she tumbled against him. As he pulled her into his arms, she felt as if she'd finally found what she'd been looking for...a place to stop, breathe, and experience that elusive peace she'd been searching for her entire life...for a week, until she and Cole both left the island to return to their lives.

How could Cole leave this place? He had his roots, his foundation, and his place of belonging? What was so wrong that he couldn't accept the place that accepted him?

10

ON CHRISTMAS MORNING, Cole leaned back in his chair at Rosie's inn, watching Willow chat with the couple seated at the same table. Rosie believed in shared tables on Christmas, and everyone was paired up with another group. They'd been matched with an older couple that he vaguely remembered from his youth. He was pretty sure they'd been coming to this island for at least twenty or thirty years.

Not that they mattered.

He just liked watching Willow. Her eyes were dancing, her smile was genuine, and her happiness was apparent. Her delight when they'd walked into Rosie's dining room had been contagious, drawing his gaze to the holiday decorations. For a brief moment, he'd been shocked into silence, stunned by the depth of his emotional response to the décor. It had thrust him directly back into his childhood, and the Christmas holidays his dad used to create at the inn. Paper snowflakes on the windows, sparkling lights tacked to the moldings, a meticulously decorated tree in the corner. The scent of fresh pine, hot coffee, and eggnog filled the air, and the faint background music of Christmas carols brought back memories he'd long forgotten. Suddenly, he was a kid again, filled with the thrill of Christmas just like he had been so long ago...all because of Willow.

She glanced over at him, and smiled, her eyes twinkling with the intimacy of a lover. He grinned back, thinking of how they'd spent the night making love until dawn. After the dance, they'd gone back to his inn, tumbled into bed, and welcomed the arrival of Christmas in each other's arms.

Best night of his damned life. If he hadn't been so determined to give Willow the Christmas she deserved, he would have skipped Rosie's and spent the day in bed, keeping Willow all to himself...but he was glad he'd brought her. The sparkle in her eyes was worth having to deal with old memories resurfacing...

He realized suddenly that the three people at his table were staring at him expectantly, waiting for his answer. "Um..." He glanced at Willow. "Sorry. I wasn't paying attention."

She rolled her eyes at him, laughing softly. "John and Susan want to buy your inn. Weren't you listening?"

He sat up quickly then. "What?"

The older gentlemen leaned forward. "We've been wanting to retire here for years, but so few properties go on the market. Your location is spectacular. You're really putting it on the market?" John's eyes were gleaming with calculating interest, and for a split second, Cole wanted to say no...except of course he wanted to sell the inn. That was why he'd come back to the island. So, he shrugged indifferently. "I'll sell it for the right price, yes."

"What's the right price?"

Cole narrowed his eyes at the eagerness in John's voice. "Make me an offer."

John leaned back in his seat, a strategic gleam in his eyes. "We'll do some research on property values, and make you an offer later today. You have a real estate agent?"

"Yep." Cole gave him the contact info for the only real estate agency on the island, all his good humor dissipating. He didn't like the proprietary gleam in their eyes, as if they were already staking a claim on his heritage. "You planning to keep it an inn?" he asked, unable to keep the edge out of his voice.

There was a long silence between the couple as they exchanged looks. Susan raised her eyebrows at her husband, and he turned back to Cole. "We might consider some enhancements," he said evasively.

Cole leaned forward, his forearms resting on the table, keeping his voice deceptively calm. "What kind of enhancements?"

"Oh, a little modernization. Things like that."

Cole narrowed his eyes, and he glanced at Willow, who was frowning at them. She looked at Cole, then turned back to the couple. "I think the property has so much potential," she said brightly. "Like a hotel, right? Or condos? It's almost ten acres, and I was telling Cole that he should sell it to someone who would build deluxe lodging there, to attract the upscale crowd. I'm sure that many of the rich and famous would like to escape here."

Cole frowned, a coldness clawing down his spine at Willow's comment. She wanted to turn this place into a second Hollywood? She'd never mentioned that to him before. Was that what she saw the island as? A place to turn into the world that had tormented her so badly?

"Oh, yes!" Susan's face lit up, and she clapped her hands with delight. "That's exactly what we were discussing! An exclusive celebrity getaway! Some would be condos, of course, and then a very upscale hotel. We could put a nice iron gate around it, and we would basically have the entire end of the island."

John put his hand on his wife's arm. "It'll cost a lot to do that," he interrupted. "So, the price would have to be right," he said, clearly trying to dumb down the price...not that Cole cared.

An elitist gated community? On the land his father had cherished? There was no chance in hell. "I think I'm done with breakfast," he said shortly. "Willow, you can see yourself back to the inn whenever you're ready."

Before she could reply, he was already to the door, anger fuming inside him. Were those his only options? Stay here and run the inn, or have it turned into some superficial elitist spa that betrayed everything that his father stood for? *Fuck.* And what the hell was up with Willow, saying she'd been telling him to do it?

"Cole?"

He spun back around to face her as she stepped out onto the front porch, pulling on the parka he'd loaned her from the stash at the inn. "What the hell was that back there?" he snapped, unable to control his fury.

Her eyes widened. "I wanted you to see what they were really like. I've spent my life around people like that, and I knew they didn't want to treasure the inn. They were going to lie to you and then tear it down after they bought it. I could see it in their eyes, so I played their game so you'd see." She frowned. "You didn't think I meant it, did you? Is that why you're mad?"

He stared at her, his mind trying to grasp her explanation. Shit. He could tell she meant it. "Sorry." He couldn't deal with this. There were so many emotions swirling around inside him, things he didn't want to deal with. "I gotta go."

"I'll go with you." She caught up to him as he strode down the steps, heading toward the main docks.

He said nothing. He just jammed his hands into his coat pockets and ignored the cold biting at his face. Willow kept up easily, jogging sometimes to stay beside him, but she didn't say anything.

He reached the end of the dock and braced his hands on the railing, staring across the bitterly cold, gray ocean. Willow stopped beside him, her hands buried in her pockets, and her stocking cap pulled down over her ears. Silence loomed between them. He didn't know what to say. He was just pissed, so fucking pissed off, and he wasn't even sure why.

"Are you rethinking your decision to sell it?" she asked finally.

He grimaced. "I can't stay. I bought a company in Australia. I'm moving there in a few days."

She looked at him sharply. "*Australia?*"

"Yeah." His fingers dug into the railing.

"Why so far away?"

"Because I hate my fucking life." The minute the words were out of his mouth, he regretted them. They sounded over-emotional and melodramatic, neither of which he was. "I mean," he clarified. "I'm ready for a different experience."

"So, you're going to run away to Australia, like you ran from here?"

He shot her a sharp glare. "You're the one running away."

"For a week! Not for my life." She touched his arm, her hand grounding him, even through his coat. "Do you even understand what you have here? The people here love you. You have this endless source of support, no matter what happens. If I had that, I'd never run away."

"That's not what this place is to me anymore." Bitterness ate away at him. "When I was seventeen, I was in love." He turned away, staring across the rough, gray sea. "Her name was Alana Rivers. Her dad was a lobsterman." Each word he spoke drummed up memories and bitterness he'd fought to forget for so long. "Lobstermen go out on the sea every day. They can't afford not to. They need the lobsters to feed their family."

Willow turned sideways to face him, propping her elbow on the railing for support.

Cole didn't face her. He just stared across the choppy water. "A storm was coming in, and it was bad. Alana asked me to go out with her and her dad so they could get through the traps faster, and get back before the storm. My mother refused to let me go. Our inn was full, and we were short on staff. She told me that the inn was more important." He swore under his breath. "Do you know how often I've heard that in my life? The inn was always open. We were responsible for our guests at all times, including me. I argued with her, and she told me if I walked out on the inn, I was betraying my father's memory. So I didn't go on the boat with them."

He ground his jaw, gripping the railing.

"What happened?" Willow's voice was quiet.

"They died." They'd fucking died. He turned to look at her then. "They got caught in the storm less than a mile off shore. They were on their way back, so close to the dock, and they got hit. The boat sank off-shore, and I was standing right here, on this dock, with my binoculars, watching it go down, and there wasn't a fucking thing I could do." He could still see it, that white boat bobbing in the brutal waters. "I could tell the minute that it stopped making progress toward the shore." He could still feel the horror stealing over him when he realized something was wrong. "I was shouting for them, but all I could do was watch. The boat went down in less than a minute. By the time I got help, it was gone. We never found their bodies. The storm took them." His eyes were burning from the cold wind. "If I'd gone with them, pulling in the traps would have taken at least an hour less. They would have been back. They would have been fine." He turned around, facing the island, glaring at the inn perched on the cliff at the north end. "That inn is the reason they died. My mom said waiting tables was more important, and I didn't fight it, so they died."

His words were ripped away by the wind, but it didn't matter. The truth was etched in blackened letters across his soul, and it would be for the rest of his life. "I hate that inn," he said softly. "I will hate it for the rest of my life."

Cole's heart felt like it was being carved in half all over again as he told the story to Willow, a story he'd never shared with anyone since that day. He'd stood in silence at their funeral, then packed up and left the island on the first ferry after his graduation. He'd come back for his mother's funeral, and then again two days ago, and it was killing him to be here.

Willow touched his arm, jerking him back to the present with sudden shock. "I'm sorry," she said softly.

A part of him wanted to grab her and pull her into his arms. He wanted to bury his face in her hair and kiss her until she chased away all the memories and guilt. But he didn't. He just shrugged and said nothing, turning back to the ocean and staring at it, trying to find his way back to the place where he didn't feel and didn't care...but he couldn't. His time with Willow had broken down his walls, and he couldn't shut off his emotions anymore.

He could almost see that white boat sinking, as if it were happening all over again. Shit. He closed his eyes, trying to cut off the image that wouldn't leave him alone. "I have to leave this behind," he finally said, bowing his head. "I can't live with this anymore."

She leaned on the railing next to him, her forearms braced on the rough wood as she watched the ocean. Her arm was against his, a solid, tangible reassurance that he was still alive. "Did it help? Leaving it behind the first time? When you moved to New York?"

He leaned on the railing beside her, keeping his arm against hers. Somehow, the casual physical contact helped ground him in the present. "Yeah. I was fine, until I had to come back here."

"Really?" Her tone made it evident that she didn't believe him at all.

He stifled a small grin at her refusal to back off, a grin that faded as he spoke. "Yeah, really."

"Because the way I see it, if your fiancée betrays you by sleeping with a friend of yours, and you feel absolutely nothing in response, then you're not okay.

You're far from okay."

What little humor he'd had fled, and he glared at her. "The fact I don't regret losing out on a cheating wife means I'm not okay? I'm smart, Willow, not weak or messed up."

"I know you're smart, and I know you're strong." She turned to face him again. "But God, Cole, look what you're doing. You're killing yourself with guilt over something that's not your fault. They made the choice to go out there—"

He ground his jaw. "They had no choice! It's the lifestyle—"

"They did have a choice! We all have a choice! You were seventeen years old! It wasn't your responsibility to take care of a grown man and force him to make the right decision to keep himself and his daughter safe! Don't you understand? You taking care of your mom and your dad's legacy didn't kill them. The storm did, and their decision to risk it. They could have cut their trip short when you couldn't come. They could have chosen not to go. They could have made a dozen different choices, and *none* of them were the responsibility of a seventeen-year-old boy!"

He stared at her. "You don't understand. You're from a movie-star life, Willow. You have no concept of what it's like to have to survive day by day like these lobstermen do."

"I understand that if you move to Australia, Alana's death will move with you. When you stare out over those beaches, you'll still see that lobster boat. It's not going to go away just because you move away. Every bad thing that happens to us is a part of us forever. It never goes away. We just incorporate it into who we are and decide who we are going to become as a result of it." She gestured toward the town center, only a few hundred yards away. "What I understand is that this place once filled your heart, and then your heart got broken horribly, first by your dad's death, and then by Alana and her dad's. You're broken, and you've rejected the only source of support you have left, so now you have nothing. That inn is all you have left of your father and a childhood filled with love, but you're letting Alana's father's decision destroy it for you."

Cole turned away from her. He felt like his head was spinning, his mind fragmenting into shattered remains. "Let it go," he said softly. "Just let it go."

"I can't."

He closed his eyes. "Why not?"

There was a moment of silence, so long that he finally turned to look at her. Her face was pale, but her eyes were burning with intensity. She took a deep breath. "I can't let it go because I love you, Cole. I can't sit here and watch you destroy yourself when you don't deserve it."

He went still, utterly frozen as her words were caught by the wind and swept past him. Her dark eyes were wide and honest as she stared at him, her cheeks flushed. Wordlessly, he touched her cheek, her skin cold from the wind. His fiancée had told him she'd loved him. So had other women. But no one had said it, and meant it, not since Alana, and they'd been kids back then. He was unprepared for what it felt like to hear it, for the way his chest tightened, and his heart sped up. It made him want to reach out and drag Willow into his arms, to grab a sword and protect her from anything bad ever coming near her. Her love, her words, her entire soul was a gift, one he didn't deserve, one that he didn't even know how to accept.

She put her hand over his. "Kiss me, Cole. Kiss me, the woman who loves you today, who sees you with all your flaws, and knows that you're the one who's worthy."

He knew he should say something, anything, but he didn't know what to say. He had no words. So, he kissed her, pouring all he was into the kiss, using it to say the words burning through him, the words that he didn't understand enough to articulate, words that could be acknowledged only by kissing Willow until he had nothing left to give.

11

*T*WO DAYS LATER, Cole appeared in the doorway to the kitchen. "That looks great."

Willow stepped back, shifting the paintbrush to her left hand to stretch her cramping fingers. Cole was wearing old jeans, faded boots, and a torn tee shirt. He looked like a man who fit perfectly into a life in Maine, working on an old house. He'd even taken off his expensive watch. His hair was tousled, his jaw was unshaven, and his shoulders were broad. He was pure testosterone, dangerous and sensual, and her heart skipped a beat at the mere sight of him. She'd spent every night in his arms, being loved in a way she'd never dreamed of. His kisses made her feel like the most beautiful woman in the world, his whispered endearments made her heart soar, and the passion between them made her soul burn for more.

She'd been on Mystic Island for six nights, and she'd never be the same. The island didn't need to trap her and keep her there. She'd found what she came for, and so much more...and with each passing moment, she felt as though it were slipping through her fingers. Soon they would be gone, the inn empty, this week nothing more than a memory, like the last time they'd been together. The thought made her heart ache, but she didn't see what other options were possible.

He had made it clear he was leaving for Australia, end of story. With a sigh, she glanced at the walls that she'd been working on all morning. "It does look nice, doesn't it?" She'd taken over painting the kitchen to prepare the inn for sale. She'd chosen a pale gray that looked almost green or blue, depending on the time of day, changing colors just like the ocean.

Cole had been cleaning out the basement all morning while she'd been painting, giving her a lot of time to think... and socialize, since Rosie and other townspeople had taken to stopping by to check on the progress and discuss ways to convince Cole not to sell the inn. They were quirky, hilarious, loyal, and always brought delicious food with them. They were all lovely, and she'd loved every minute of painting, chatting, and turning something old and worn out into something vibrant and alive.

Nighttime had been for lovemaking with Cole, and she'd fallen more in love with him every passing moment. She now understood the depth of his trauma, and she knew he believed he had to walk away from the inn. There was simply no other way he could heal, but his fury at the possibility of it being torn down in betrayal of his father's legacy had been revealing. Was it really the right choice for him to sell it? He hadn't talked much about his mother, and it was clear that his dad was the one Cole had been close to, even before his mom had gotten remarried. Without his dad to hold them together, the relationship between him and his mom had gradually decayed over time.

His memories of life after his father's death had destroyed his love for what had once mattered to him. It made her sad for him, but she had begun to understand there was no way to change his mind.

He was going to leave on that ferry and never come back.

"It's a great shade of gray." He leaned on the doorframe, and ran his hand across his forehead, leaving streaks of dust. He was so far from the boy she'd known. He was pure male, wildly sexy and deeply emotional, so much more than he would let himself acknowledge. "My dad would have loved that color."

She smiled at the softness in his voice, the same warm tone he always used when talking about his dad. "He sounds like he would have loved a lot of what you've been doing here this week," she ventured as she resumed painting. "You've restored so much of the inn's ambiance even in this short week. It feels like guests could arrive any minute, doesn't it?"

Cole didn't answer. He just leaned against the doorframe, watching her silently.

After a moment, she looked over at him. His eyes were turbulent, his jaw tense. She paused. "What?"

"I just wanted to apologize that you didn't get much of a Christmas," he said. "I hope you didn't feel obligated to help me get things in shape. You came here for Christmas, and you wound up painting my house."

She smiled, touched by his concern. This was the man who prided himself on being cold? He'd given her a wonderful Christmas, enveloped her in lovemaking every night, and had invited her into his private, solitary world all week, and yet he was still concerned about her well-being? "I've had the best time," she said honestly. "My whole life has been expensive hotels and staff who take care of anything I need. I love painting. I love helping you in the kitchen and learning how to cook. I love everything about this week." *Including you.* She wanted to tell him again that she loved him, but she was afraid of breaking the spell that had been woven between them.

His eyebrows rose up. "You mean that? You really like it here?"

"I do." She bit her lip, then put down the brush and turned to face him, finally saying what had been weighing on her with a mounting heaviness for the last day. "The ferry comes tomorrow." Tomorrow. Tomorrow. Tomorrow. This would all be over tomorrow.

Something flickered in his eyes, an emotion so fleeting that she didn't have a chance to identify it. He nodded. "I know."

"The house isn't done." *The house wasn't done?* Really? *That* was what she was going to say about leaving tomorrow? That the house wasn't finished? What about the fact that she felt as though her heart was shattering at the idea of leaving behind the intimacy of this week with Cole, and the connection she had with the island already? What about the fact that she'd fallen madly, deeply, and hopelessly in love with him? What about the fact that she felt like leaving here would break both their hearts, not just hers, even if he refused to see it? Those were the things that mattered, the things she wanted to say…but she didn't dare express them. Cole had made it so clear that he was moving to Australia. Telling him how sad she was to leave him and the island would accomplish nothing, except making her vulnerable again.

He glanced around, taking in the freshly painted walls, the dusted furniture, and the polished floors. "It'll be good enough, I think. You can feel the charm of the building again. It feels like it matters now. People will feel the magic of it when they come in." He ran his hand over the glistening doorframe. "The magic is back," he said softly. "Can't you feel it?"

"I can." How could he walk away from this? She knew it mattered to him. If it didn't, he'd never be able to talk about magic and how the inn mattered. She tried again. "How are you going to keep someone from buying it who will tear it down?"

He shrugged, his voice cool as he dropped his hand from the wall. "I decided it doesn't matter. It's just a building."

"No!" She leapt to her feet. "You don't mean that! There's so much life and so many memories in this building! It would be horrible to have it torn down and made into impersonal condos!"

He gave her a steady gaze, his jaw taut. "Maybe it's okay. Maybe that's what needs to happen. Rip the past from its foundation and let it float out to sea."

"Dammit, Cole! What is wrong with you?" She tossed the paintbrush into the can, ignoring the paint that splattered over her jeans as she leapt to her feet. "For God's sake, why can't you see what's so special about this building? How can you look at it and just see the bad, when you had so much good here? Why do you have to let the shadows win?"

His eyes glittered. "If you like it so much, why don't you buy it?"

She stared at him in shock. "What?"

"I said—"

"I know what you said." Her mind began to whirl

with ideas, dozens and dozens flooding her mind. Did she dare? Was she ready to really walk away from her life forever? To give up on the chance that someday her ticket to celebrity would finally be punched? She looked around at the kitchen, with its drop cloths, hand-carved table, and old buoys perched on top of the cabinets. She didn't know anything about running an inn, or being a chef, or even owning a business...but the idea made her heart flutter with excitement. She whirled around to face him. "Would you teach me?"

He frowned. "Teach you what?"

"How to run it? If I bought it? Could I call you if I bought it? With questions?" The moment she asked it, she suddenly realized what she'd said...calling Cole meant taking things past this week...and calling him was a sobering reminder that he would be in Australia, gone from her life. Did she really want to live here without Cole? Was *he* the reason she was so happy here? Or was there more?

He blinked. "You want to buy it?" he asked slowly.

Did she? Did she really want to? Did she want to commit her life here? "I...I..." She broke off, staring at him. "I don't know." If he would stay, if they could do it together, then it would be an absolute, without a doubt, yes. But alone? Would the island soon seem small and confining if she didn't have Cole by her side? "Would you...consider staying? If I bought it? For a while?"

He stared at her for a long time, and he shook his head.

"Okay, right, of course you wouldn't." She turned away to hide her disappointment.

"Hey." Cole was suddenly beside her, his fingers on her elbow. "Willow."

She glanced at him. "What?"

"You need to understand something," he said, his voice low and intense. "If there were anyone or anything that could keep me here, it would be you. You make me want to breathe again. You make me want to smile, the kind of smile that's for real, not for show." He slipped his hand around hers, squeezing gently. "You make me wish that I could turn back time and keep you the first time, when I might still have been capable of loving you the way you deserved. You make me wish I had the ability to put myself out there and love again."

Tears burned in her eyes. "You do have the ability to love, Cole. You just have to be willing to feel again. You can't have love without being willing to get hurt."

"I wish it was that simple." He pulled her against him and kissed her, the kind of tender, intimate kiss that told her he was lying to himself that he couldn't love. He could...if he made that choice.

But she knew he wouldn't.

This was all he could give, one week of his life before he left. She knew her heart would break when she said good-bye to him. She'd never felt loved before, and she'd never loved someone so deeply. She felt alive, and that was why she'd come to Mystic Island. He'd given her back her life...and he was going to break her heart.

He wrapped his arm around her and dragged her against him, pouring his emotions into the kiss—

Her phone rang, and she tensed, surprised. Her phone hadn't rung once since she'd arrived in Maine.

"Don't answer it," he muttered, sliding his lips over the side of her neck. "This is our last night. Let's let reality intrude tomorrow." His kiss took away any chance she had at resisting. And he was right. Tomorrow would come soon enough.

* * *

Cole woke up to find his bed empty. The sun was just starting to break across the sky, and he swore at the sudden weight in his chest. This was it. The week was over. He'd never set foot on the island again. He knew he should be happy, but he felt like he was drowning. Because he was leaving the island, or leaving Willow? Swearing, he rolled onto his side to get up and find her, then realized she was sitting on the side of the bed, her phone in her hand.

She was wearing one of his shirts, and her hair was tousled from a night of lovemaking. She looked achingly beautiful, and he knew he'd never see anything that would touch him more deeply than the vision of Willow sitting on his bed, with the golden rays of dawn streaking across her face. For a split second, he imagined what it would be like to wake up with her every day, to tackle the inn together, to see her smiling face bring joy to everyone she met. Would she be enough to take away the pain? Would she be able to heal him? To bring peace to the nightmares that still haunted him? What if he stayed? What if they stayed together? Could she chase away the shadows that never let him go? Could she make the inn a place of happiness again, the way it had once been?

Then she turned to him, and he saw something in her eyes that made his heart stop. Anguish. "What happened?"

She held up her phone. "You know that call I didn't answer last night?"

"Yeah." He sat up. "What was it?"

"You know the Dark Phantom trilogy that they're starting to film? Based on that fantasy series?"

He frowned. "Yes, of course."

"They're two weeks into filming in Ireland, and the lead actress just got carted off to rehab. She's out of the film." She met his gaze. "They're desperate to find someone who has no other commitments for the next year and a half of filming, they're way over budget, and they need someone who doesn't cost much, but who carries enough clout in Hollywood to get fans." She held out her hands in a shrug. "Guess who?"

He stared at her, processing her words as the image of the two of them running the inn faded away. "You got it?" He wanted to be thrilled for her, but he had the sense of something precious slipping away, just out of his reach. He wanted to lunge for her, grab her, and find a way to keep the world at bay, but instead, he just sat there, struggling to find the equilibrium that had suddenly abandoned him.

"Yeah. They're sending a helicopter in an hour. Apparently, they can land on the dock."

"Yes, it's where life-flight comes when they need to take someone to the mainland." He frowned, struggling to process the situation. Her brow was furrowed, and she looked anguished. "You're not happy? Isn't that what you've wanted your whole life? This is your break. They're already talking about all the major awards for this movie."

"Yes." She sighed. "But last night, after we made love the second time. I was lying awake in your arms, listening to the creaks of the house, and I knew I didn't want to leave. I made the decision to buy the inn. I know you won't stay, and that made it harder because it's you that makes me so happy, but when I thought about it, I knew this was right for me."

Something inside him turned over, and suddenly, he couldn't breathe. "You're going to stay? And buy the inn?"

"I was." She held up her phone. "But then this happened. How do I turn this down? How do I walk away from a chance for the career I've always wanted?"

It took him a full minute to pull his shit together and formulate an answer. He wanted to tell her not to take it. He wanted to tell her to turn it down, and stay on the island with him, and run the inn...except he couldn't make that offer. He couldn't stay there anymore than she could, and he sure as hell couldn't drag her into a forever with a cold, uncaring bastard when she could have her dreams instead. "You don't turn it down." Hell, the words actually hurt his throat as he said them. "You'd never forgive yourself." He leaned forward, and took her hands in his. They were cold and trembling, and her eyes were wide with fear. Her apprehension seemed to settle his own anguish, chased away by his need to be her foundation, the rock she didn't have in her life. "This is your chance to show the world how amazing you are in your own right. You'll nail it, and you'll change the world. There's no way you can pass it up. You'll regret it forever."

She searched his face. "Just like you regretted it forever when you let the inn keep you from going out on that boat?"

"Forever is a long time to regret something," he said, not directly answering the question. He let out his breath and ran his hand through her hair. "You deserve this, Willow. You've found your place. Go out and show the world who you are. You can do it."

She nodded, tears brimming in her eyes. "I love

you," she whispered. "I would have stayed here with you and run the inn. I would still choose you if you'd ask." She searched his face, looking for the answers that he wanted to give her so desperately.

I would have stayed here, too. The words burned in his mind, but he didn't say them. It was too late. He wouldn't be the reason she gave up on her dream. So, instead, he simply shook his head. "I wouldn't have stayed," he lied.

Her face fell, and something inside his gut twisted. Shit. He couldn't let her go without the truth...or at least part of it. She deserved it. "But I was wrong earlier," he said. "When I said I couldn't love you." He took a deep breath. "I love you, Willow Morgan, with every bit of my scarred and twisted heart, I love you."

Tears filled her eyes. "Cole—"

He didn't let her finish, instead bringing her hand to his lips and pressing a kiss to her knuckles. "When you get on that helicopter, I want you to remember that you're loved the way you deserve. Hold that with you no matter what happens, and know that I believe in you, no matter how hard it gets. Got it?"

She searched his face. "You love me?"

"Yeah. I do. It's not much, but it's all I have." He kissed her again, drinking in the taste of her lips, the feel of her body against his, her familiar scent. Too fucking bad for him that he'd found her *now*, that it had taken this long for him to finally figure out that what he really wanted was a lifetime with her. He'd never stand in her way. He'd never let her live a lifetime of regret the way he had.

And the way she kissed him back told him that she also knew that what they had would never be found again.

12

WILLOW PRESSED HER fingers to the window of the helicopter, watching Cole as he stood in the midst of the small crowd that had come out to see what the helicopter was all about. Rosie was standing beside him, but Willow could look only at Cole. His hair was whipping from the helicopter, and his hands were shoved deep in the pockets of his overcoat. He was dressed for work, not for the inn, and he looked every bit the executive who was hopping on the ferry in an hour to go run his business. He didn't look like the man in jeans that he'd become during the week. He looked like the man she'd met on the ferry a week ago, and that made her heart break.

"Why didn't you ask me to stay?" she whispered, leaning her forehead against the window. But she knew the answer. He loved her, but he couldn't stay. Could she have stayed without him? Would she really have bought the inn and given up her life?

She'd never know now.

It was over.

The helicopter lifted off the dock, and tears rolled down her cheeks as she watched him get smaller and smaller, until she couldn't see him anymore. So, instead, she watched the inn as they flew away, until that, too, disappeared from sight.

Her hands were shaking as she leaned back in her seat and the enormity of what she was facing finally hit her. She was going to anchor the franchise that the entire industry had been anticipating ever since the movie deal had been announced. Could she really do it? Before this week, she wouldn't have believed it, but Cole had changed her. The people of Mystic Island had changed her. They believed in her because of who she was, not because of her family. Cole's love had showed her that she was worthy, amazing, and capable. Cole had taught her to love herself, exactly as she was, and that was an incredible gift.

She'd said she'd come to the island to feel alive again, and not for love. She'd gotten what she'd wanted, and the island had let her go. Until the last minute when the island had disappeared from sight, she'd been half-expecting something to happen that would keep her from leaving, the way it had in the legends. But no storm had arisen. The helicopter had arrived, and the island had let her go…which meant that her experience was complete.

So, why did she feel so empty?

She slipped her fingers into the pocket of her jacket, and pulled out the tiny wreath Cole had woven for her, clutching it in her hand. "I love you, Cole," she whispered.

The only answer was the roar of the helicopter.

* * *

She was gone.

Cole stood alone on the main dock, watching the helicopter until it vanished from the horizon, a black speck that blinked out of sight. He didn't move for a long time, watching the last spot he'd seen it, as if he could will it to reappear and bring Willow back to him.

But it didn't. The sky was blue, beautiful, and so empty he felt as if it were a gaping chasm that had stolen his soul, just like the ocean had done so long ago. Except this time, it was so much more, a raw, searing loss that made his soul feel like it was shattering into a thousand pieces. Willow had taken a piece of his heart with her, and it fucking hurt.

He hadn't come to the island to regain his ability to feel. He hadn't come to morph into some sensitive guy who could feel every crack in his heart. He'd come to purge himself of the albatross of his past so he could walk away and never look back. Instead, he'd come alive...and then felt pain almost as cutting as when his father had died...before he'd learned to shut it down.

Willow had broken his shields, and he wanted them back. It fucking hurt to care, and she'd opened the wounds to his past until he felt like he couldn't breathe, he was so sunken in the pain of so much loss.

He hadn't been able to stop his dad from dying.

He hadn't been able to rescue Alana from the ocean.

But he knew that he could have stopped Willow from leaving. He'd seen in her eyes that she would have stayed if he'd asked. He'd wanted to. His need to keep her had burned through every cell in his body. Losing her had ripped open all the scars that had protected him for so long. He'd wanted to stop her from leaving. He'd wanted to tell her to stay. He'd wanted to make her the kind of promises he'd never made anyone in his life. He'd wanted to keep her so badly, and he'd known in his gut that he could have kept her if he'd spoken up...but he'd had to let her go.

He loved her too much to take away her future. The only acceptable choice had been to step back and encourage her to embrace her chance to have the dream she'd fought for her entire life, but it fucking sucked.

"Cole."

He stiffened at the familiar voice, the one he hadn't heard in so long, the last one he wanted to hear right now. He swore under his breath, trying to pull his emotions together and school his features into an impassive expression. It took several seconds before he'd steeled himself, and then he turned his head.

Beside him stood Paul Rickman, his mother's second husband, the man who'd stepped into his father's role without a second of hesitation, the man who had once been the best friend of Cole's dad. Paul's hair was gray now, thinning, but his shoulders were erect and strong. His heavy jacket was zipped all the way up, and his hands were shoved deep in his pockets. He looked old now, old and worn. Cole hadn't spoken to him at his mother's funeral, keeping to himself, and letting Paul direct the services. But there was no way to avoid him now. He inclined his chin in acknowledgement. "Paul."

"Hurts, doesn't it?"

Cole cleared his throat, trying to find a way to shut down the grief thundering through him. "What hurts?"

"Saying good-bye to the woman you love."

Cole flexed his jaw. "Yeah, well, it happens." He

didn't want to have this conversation. He wanted to get away from the island that seemed to do nothing more than give him someone to love and take them away. The magic of the island was bullshit. It was a place where hell won.

"You have a sec?"

Cole let out his breath, then turned to face the older man. "Paul, I'll be honest. I'm not much in the mood to talk. The ferry comes in an hour, and I need to get packed up."

"Then I'll talk, and I'll make it quick." Paul looked right at him, his pale gray eyes the same color as the ocean on a stormy day. "You were a kid before, but you're a man now, and it's time you heard it."

Foreboding rippled through Cole. There was no way he was going to revisit his dad's death or anything related to it. "It's over, Paul. It's long over. Let it lie." He wasn't in the mood to hear some sort of confession about how he'd loved Cole's mom long before his dad had died.

"No, it's not." Paul held out an envelope, one that was tattered and worn, yellowing on the corners. "This is for you."

Cole shoved his hands into his jacket pockets. "I don't want it. I don't need it."

"Your dad wrote it."

Cole went cold, staring at the battered envelope. "My dad?" he echoed blankly, staring at the weathered paper.

"A month before he died. Take it."

Slowly, Cole took the envelope from Paul's hand. He was surprised to see his hand was shaking. He turned away, walking to the edge of the dock, before he opened it. He recognized his dad's handwriting immediately, and his gut clenched. It was as if his dad had suddenly come back to life for a final good-bye, and it shook Cole hard. It took a minute for his eyes to clear enough to read the faded writing. *Paul. I need you to take care of my boy. He's going to have it rough after I'm gone. He and his mom don't get along that well. He's going to need someone. You're my best friend. I need this from you. Promise me.*

Cole closed his eyes against the surge of emotion. He felt as though his dad had reached down from heaven and rested his hand on his shoulder, just as he'd done so many times before. *Dad.*

"I promised him I'd protect you," Paul said, walking up beside him. "I thought marrying your mom was the best way to do it, but I was wrong."

Cole's throat was tight, and he had to clear it several times before he could speak. "You married my mom because of your promise to my dad? I thought...I thought you...people said that you and my mom were having an affair before my dad died." He glanced over at Paul. "I thought that all the time you spent at our place had actually been to see my mom."

Paul sighed. "I'm not going to lie, Cole. I grew to love her deeply. She was an amazing woman, and an incredible mother to my boys. I cherished every minute with her." Paul leaned on the railing, staring across the ocean "Your mom and I talked about it after your dad's funeral. We both decided it was the right choice. She was devastated by your dad's death and wanted to keep his legacy going for your sake, but she couldn't afford to run the inn herself. She was worried about you, aware that you and she didn't have a strong bond. The day we decided to get married, it was as friends, not lovers. We didn't fall in love until later."

Cole's fingers closed around the envelope, cradling the old paper carefully, his mind spinning as he processed everything Paul was telling him. "You paid the expenses of the inn?" he asked. "You kept it going for my dad?"

"Yeah. It was important to him that you didn't lose it. He knew what it meant to you, but he was short on cash. It never ran much of a profit, and your mom was going to have to sell it. It was never her first love, as you know. It was your dad's baby."

Cole closed his eyes, remembering, for the first time in ages, how proud he'd been the first time he'd cooked dinner for the guests, with his dad's oversight. He recalled admiring their work after they'd repainted the exterior. He remembered watching guests sip cocktails on the deck he'd rebuilt with his father. His mom had kept the inn *for him*, not because she wanted it? No wonder she'd closed on Christmas after she'd married Paul. It hadn't been because Paul had taken her away from it. It was because she'd never loved it in the first place, but she'd kept it going *for him*. His throat tightened, and he ran his hands through his hair as the constructs he'd believed in for so long came tumbling down around him.

"I couldn't help you," Paul said softly. "I did everything I could think of to reach you, but you hated everything about me. Every night when I go to sleep, I think about how I've failed your dad and you."

Cole gritted his jaw, trying to think through the rush of emotions flooding him. So much he hadn't known, so much he'd been wrong about for so long. "Why didn't you tell me the truth?"

Paul looked at him, and for the first time, Cole saw the weariness in the man's eyes. "Would you have believed me?"

Cole let out his breath, and thought back to who he'd been back then. Angry. Bitter. Isolated. He'd hated the inn. He'd resented his mother. He'd hated Paul for betraying his dad, and for being the one who was still alive. "No." If Paul had tried to explain, Cole probably would have torn up the letter without even reading it, and it would have been gone forever.

He turned toward the ocean, and leaned on the railing next to Paul. For a long while, he struggled with what to say, to find words that would chase away all the dirt of their past. Finally, he said simply, "I'm sorry."

Paul glanced over at him. "No apologies, Cole. We all live as best we can."

"Do we? Or do we look for the shit just so we can bury ourselves in it?" He was pissed now, angry at the kid he'd once been, aware of how much lost time had passed over the years, time when he could have kept his father's memory alive through Paul.

"Some of both, I think."

They both fell silent, and the only sound was the crashing of the waves against the pilings of the dock. Cole listened to the rush of water, a sound he hadn't listened to in so long. He let himself notice the rich, loamy scent of the ocean, and the taste of the salty air on his lips, the things that had once been such a part of him that they'd been a part of the fabric of his soul.

"Do yourself a favor, Cole," Paul said after a bit. "Don't give up living because you're trying to run from the past. It'll go with you wherever you go, no matter how far you go."

Cole managed a grim smile. "Willow said the same thing."

"Smart woman."

Again, silence fell between them, but for the first time since his dad's death, Cole felt like some of the shadows that had been haunting him were lighter. "Thanks for trying so hard all that time, Paul. You didn't need to do it." He looked over his shoulder at the inn standing so proudly on the bluff that overlooked the town. "Thanks for saving the inn," he added quietly.

"I'll keep trying to help you until I'm dead. That promise to your dad is forever."

Cole's throat tightened, and he ran his finger over the worn envelope. "How many times have you read this?"

"Every day. I wanted to make sure I never forgot, even a little." Paul continued to look across the ocean. "I was planning to talk to you at your mom's funeral, but I wasn't in the right place. My heart broke the day she died, and when I saw you across the church, with the same eyes as hers, I felt like you were my last connection with either of them, a connection that I hadn't been able to save. It hurt to look at you, son. Your dad was my best friend, and your mom made my heart beat. You're my only connection to them, and I was afraid that if I spoke to you that day, I'd break the last thread that connected me to those I'd lost."

Cole let out his breath, his chest constricting at the pain in the older man's voice. "I'm sorry for judging you."

Paul smiled. "It's what teenagers do. My boys would have been in much worse shape if your mom hadn't been there for them. I always felt guilty that by marrying her, I wound up taking her away from you instead of giving you the support I intended."

Cole shook his head. "My mom and I never got along. That wouldn't have changed no matter what." He shifted restlessly. "I did miss my dad, though. I still do."

"I know. I do, too. Every day." Paul chuckled. "I'll never forget the day he grabbed the microphone at the Christmas party and sang *Silent Night.*"

Cole laughed, picturing his dad on the stage. "I forgot about that. Too much eggnog. He was God-awful up there."

Paul laughed too, reminding Cole of the days he'd sit around with Paul and his dad after dinner on the front porch, enjoying the night while the guests retired. Those had been good days, days long gone. But maybe, just maybe, new ones could be formed. "You want to get a coffee?" he asked. "My treat."

Paul raised his brows. "Yeah, I would."

Cole smiled. "You pick the place. I'm a little out of touch."

"The best is still The Mermaid Cafe. You up for it?"

It had been his dad's favorite place. "Yeah, I am. Let's go."

13

*W*ILLOW STOOD AT the edge of the movie set in Ireland, watching everyone race around as they prepared for the day's shooting. It was a scene so familiar to her, one she'd grown up around. As familiar as it was, however, it was also completely different, because this time, she belonged here by her own right. It was her set. Not her mom's. Not her dad's. Hers.

She'd felt the difference the moment she'd stepped out of the limo. The director had been waiting for her to welcome her personally. She'd been assigned a personal assistant to get her anything she wanted, no matter what it was. She had her own trailer, with her name emblazoned across the door in gold and black letters. It was everything she'd aspired to for so long.

But when she saw that deluxe trailer with her name, the thought that had flashed through her mind was how ugly it was compared to Cole's inn. When she'd gone to sleep at night, her bed had felt cold and empty. When someone had hammered on her door to demand her appearance, she'd thought of Rosie's friendly visits. Even now, as she stood with her perfectly coifed hair and her scene-appropriate makeup, she felt a deep sense of wrongness, not the satisfaction she'd expected.

Why didn't this feel right? Why didn't it feel the way it was supposed to? This was her world, and now she'd finally claimed her spot...and yet she didn't want to be here.

She hated the way everyone called her Ms. Morgan. The paparazzi were haunting her, just as they had her whole life, still looking for that horrible moment they could expose her to the world. Her co-star had made it clear that he was making the film under protest, because he'd signed on to co-star with an A-list actress, not an untalented Hollywood legacy who got the job because of her last name. He'd made it clear that it *wasn't* her set. She was just a last choice when no one else could do it.

She'd known she'd been a last resort, of course, because she wasn't an idiot. But now that she was here, the enormity of what she'd taken on had settled down upon her. The pressure was extraordinary to deliver a top-level performance in such a highly anticipated film. She knew she could do it. She knew she was doing good work, and she knew she'd pull it off, no matter what her co-star thought. This chance to prove herself was what she'd fought for her entire life, but now that she'd attained it, it was an empty victory. It wasn't any better being a star than it was being the untalented offspring of stars. It was the same, and she didn't want to be here. The glitz and the glam wasn't her. It hadn't been when she'd been on the fringes, and it wasn't now that she was in the midst of it.

She wanted to be on Mystic Island, living a life that mattered to her, with people who mattered to her. With Cole.

She sighed at the thought of the man she hadn't been able to stop thinking about since she'd left. She missed him more than she could ever grasp. She missed his smile, his frown, and the mischievous gleam in his eye when he decided it was time for them to take an extended break from painting. She missed the way he believed in her. She missed how he made her feel like the most special, most loved woman in the world. She missed everything about him, and the island he'd once called home.

She didn't want to be here. She wanted to be there, and she wanted to be there now. For good.

The moment she thought it, she realized it was true. This wasn't her world. Her world was elsewhere, and she just hadn't been brave enough to take it. Maybe Cole wasn't going to stay and run the inn with her, but that didn't mean she had to live the life she didn't want. Her heart pounding, she pulled her phone out of her pocket, and hit the auto-dial for her agent, excitement mounting with each ring. Her agent finally answered. "Willow—"

"I'm dropping out of the movie." Excitement leapt through her, and she couldn't stop grinning. She felt so strong, so empowered, the most liberated she'd felt in her entire life.

"What? You can't! You signed a contract!"

"Everyone on the set will be thrilled, trust me. It's not a fit. I'm out."

"You'll never work again in this business," he warned.

She laughed at his melodrama, relief rushing

through her. "I know. Thank God, right?"

"What? Willow—"

She hung up and hugged the phone to her chest, unable to stop the smile from spreading across her face. And just like that, it was over. A lifetime of wanting to be a part of something that never fit her. She was finally free.

"Hiding in the shadows like this is somewhat anti-social, you know," a familiar voice whispered in her ear.

"Cole!" She whirled around to find him standing behind her, looking so deliciously handsome and wonderful that tears filled her eyes. He was wearing jeans, boots, and a flannel shirt untucked from his jeans. He looked like a rugged Maine man, sexy, untamed, and wonderful. Without stopping to think, she flung her arms around him, burying herself against him.

He hugged her tightly, pulling them further into the shadows as he kissed her, a desperate, intense kiss that enveloped her so completely it was as if they'd never been apart.

"God, I missed you," he whispered.

"Me, too." She wrapped her arms around him, unable to keep the smile off her face. She grinned up at him, giddy with happiness that he was there. "I thought you'd be on your way to Australia by now."

He shrugged and fingered her overly styled hair with a frown. "I missed my ferry, so I was stuck on the island for another week, which made me miss my flight. So, I painted some walls. Hung out with Luc and his son. Stalked Rosie. Did some thinking." He enfolded her hands in his, drawing her against him. "Here's the thing, Willow. You were right."

She grinned at him, too happy to see him to care

what he was talking about. "Right about what?"

"The past becoming a part of you. I got off the plane here, and I could still see that boat sinking. It didn't go away. It will never go away. Neither will the pain of losing my dad. Running from the island didn't make it go away."

She nodded, her smile fading. "I know. It never does."

"But it did start to fade when I was stuck on that island for that extra week. I talked to people I hadn't talked to in a long time. I went to my parents' graves. I went to the graves of Alana and her dad. I made peace with my stepdad, and even hung out with my stepbrothers."

Her throat tightened. She could see the peace in his eyes, peace that had never been there before. "I'm so glad, Cole. But...why are you here? You could have called me to tell me."

"Yeah, but this is better." He raised her hands and pressed a kiss to her knuckle. "I can't sell the inn, Willow. It's my family's legacy, and mine. I want to keep it. I want to run it. I want my kids to grow up there."

She smiled, her heart lifting at the image he painted. "I'm so glad to hear that—"

"But," he said, interrupting her. "That means you can't buy it. I felt kind of bad about that, because I know you wanted to, so I wanted to make you a deal."

Something in the gleam of his eye made her heart quicken. "A deal? What kind of deal might that be?"

"Well, see, here's the thing." His eyes were glinting with that same teasing mischievousness she'd missed. "I enjoyed being at the inn over Christmas, but this week, without you, was kind of rough. So, I thought maybe you'd want to run it with me? Sort of a tag team effort?"

Her grin widened, but she couldn't stop from teasing him right back. "What are you saying? That you want to hire me as a manager?"

His expression became serious, his gaze intense. "No. I want you to be my partner, in every way." He traced his fingers along her jaw, in an intimate gesture that made her heart ache with longing. "I'll sell my company in Australia. I didn't want it anyway. I can fly back and forth between here and Mystic Island, and when you're on break between movies, you can come back there with me. It's a long distance thing, but we can make it work."

Her heart seemed to stand still, and suddenly she couldn't breathe. "Really?"

He nodded, his fingers tightening on hers. "If you don't want to fly, that's fine. I'm happy to do all the traveling. I've lost too many people I love, and I'm not losing you. Whatever it takes, I'll do it."

Her throat tightened, and sudden doubt flickered through her. "What if I was just me? What if I wasn't a movie star? Would you still feel that way?"

Cole laughed softly. "You really have to ask that, sweetheart? You know that you're the one I love. I've loved you since you were fifteen. Not your last name. Not your family. I love you. Why would you even ask that?"

Her throat tightened, and tears filled her eyes. "Because I just quit. I don't have a job anymore, and in about five minutes, they're going to boot me off the set."

"You quit?" At her nod, he frowned. "You want to walk away from this? It's your dream."

"No. It's the dream of other people." She laced her

fingers behind his neck and leaned into him, basking in the feel of his strong body against hers. Never had a place felt right before, but being in Cole's arms was overwhelmingly perfect. "It's the dream I was told I had to want. I have it, and I hate it. I hate everything about being here, just like I hated it when I was a kid."

"Are you certain?" Cole searched her face. "This is your chance to be a superstar, Willow. You've made it. You don't have to choose. I'll make it work. I don't want you to make this sacrifice for me."

She shook her head. "I'm positive, Cole. I know what I want, and what makes me happy now. I thought it had to be in front of a camera, because that's all I knew. But it's not. It's with you, on a small island off the coast of Maine, with people who care about each other and stand beside each other." She smiled. "A place where Christmas matters."

A smile lit up his face, the most beautiful smile she'd ever seen. "You made me believe in Christmas again, sweetheart. I don't want to face another one without you. If you come home with me, I'm never going to let you go. You realize that, don't you? Every Christmas is going to be with me, at that inn, helping other people find what it brought us."

"I'm counting on it." She beamed at him. "You taught me what Christmas is all about, and that's being with those who matter. Like you."

"Like you," Cole repeated. "I love you, Willow." And then he kissed her, and this time, it wasn't a kiss of good-bye. It was a kiss of shared dreams, healed hearts, and the promise of forever.

* * *

"They're coming up the walkway! Are you ready?"

Willow raced into the kitchen, stripping off her apron. Her eyes were glowing, her hair was in a loose pony-tail, and she was wearing the diamond earrings Cole had commissioned from a local artist on the island. The diamonds were framed by scallop shells made of white gold, which were dangling from a hoop designed to look like twisted twigs, immortalizing both their first kiss, and their second one years later.

They'd come out perfectly, and he'd been too pleased by them to wait for Christmas. Instead, he'd used Thanksgiving as an excuse, and surprised her earlier in the day, when they'd first woken up. She'd cried, and he'd gotten a little tight in his throat. They weren't just earrings. They memorialized the connection between them, the one that had endured over time and distance, until it had finally healed both their hearts.

Cole grinned as they sparkled on her ears, his heart tightening at the sight of them. He hadn't been emotional or sentimental before they'd met, but she'd changed that for him. She'd changed everything for him.

Willow's face softened when she noticed his gaze was on the earrings. "Cole, they're beautiful. I'll treasure them always."

"I know." He pulled her in for a quick kiss. "They just remind me of how you saved me. I love you, sweetheart."

She wrapped her arms around his neck, melting into him, as she always did whenever he reached out for her. "I love you, too. Always and forever. Tell me again how you believe in the magic of Mystic Island? I love being right."

He laughed and kissed the tip of her nose. "I chose to miss that ferry. The island didn't keep me here. I made the choice myself." When her brows knit in a frown, he laughed again. "Okay, I admit it. The island brought us together when we needed to find each other. I believe in love, and I believe in magic, and I believe in the island." The truth was, he did believe. Nothing else but magic could explain how he'd been lucky enough to find Willow.

The front door slammed and he heard Paul call out. "Happy Thanksgiving! Anyone around? I heard there's a Charbonneau holiday special going on the table tonight!"

"Come on back," Cole called out. "We're in the kitchen!"

"They're here!" Willow's eyes lit up, grabbing his arms. "I'm so excited. I told them all that it was my first Thanksgiving dinner, and I might ruin everything, but they didn't care."

"That's because they knew I had your back. I'm the best chef on the island. Everyone knows it." He nodded at the oven. "Turkey's almost done. We're all set."

"I'll go greet them!" Willow started to head for the door, but Cole grabbed her arm and hauled her back against him.

"Just a minute," he said, pulling her in for one last kiss, needing that connection with her, as he always did. She smiled, her face soft with understanding of how much he needed her. She melted against him, and it wasn't until he heard the catcalls from their guests that he broke the kiss.

Willow pulled away, her cheeks flushed with embarrassment and happiness as she welcomed everyone into the kitchen. Paul, along with his three sons, who Cole had gotten to know again. Luc was there, with his son, while Rosie and her second, wonderful husband rounded it out. He and Willow had scheduled dinner late in the evening, after Rosie had served her guests. Since she was the one who had sent Willow to Cole's inn during the storm, she held a special place in their lives, especially tonight.

Cole grinned as greetings and hugs were exchanged. He thudded Luc on the back, glad that his friend could make it. He had a feeling Luc and his son would have had a pretty simple Thanksgiving if they hadn't joined them, and he was glad for the chance to add some holiday spirit to their table. He grinned at the thought, realizing he was thinking just like his dad used to, and it felt good.

He greeted Rosie and the others, then shook Paul's hand. "Glad you could make it."

"Wouldn't miss it. It's been a long time since we've had Thanksgiving dinner here," Paul grinned. "Are you really opening up for Christmas this year?"

"Yep. The upgrades are almost done. The place needed a lot more work than we thought." He was damn proud of all that he and Willow had accomplished. He'd hired out the electrician, but the rest they'd done themselves. He could have paid for someone to do it, but it had felt so much better to do it themselves, creating memories with Willow as the inn came to life. "We're going to need a handyman to help with things once we open. You interested?" He and Willow had decided to do the inn a little differently, and to make sure it didn't consume them. Now that Paul was retired from the hardware store, they'd both felt that it was a perfect solution to bring him on board.

The older man's face lit up. "Really? I'd love to."

"You're hired then." He grinned as Paul immediately turned to his sons and told them, his lined face creased with happiness.

Satisfaction filled Cole as he opened a bottle of wine he'd found in the wine cellar. It was a vintage Chardonnay, the last bottle of his dad's favorite wine. He'd saved it for tonight. It felt right to honor his dad with their first holiday in the inn. The table was set with the finest china in the main dining room, but it felt natural to have everyone hanging out in the kitchen, like they used to do in the old days.

Willow gave him her special, warm smile as he handed her the bottle, and she began pouring with the flair of someone who'd been doing it her whole life. "I'm so excited for the guests to start arriving on December first," she declared. "I mean, I'm nervous, but I'm excited, too. It was so wonderful to see how the guests were eager to book reservations again, even though the inn had been closed."

Cole grinned, stepping back to watch the room as everyone fell into easy conversation. It was like being a kid again, only it was different now, because now he appreciated every minute of it. There was just one thing left to make it right. He tapped his wine glass to get people's attention.

The small crowd stopped talking and turned toward him.

"I wanted to thank you all for coming, and for sticking by me all these years. I'm glad to be back." Everyone raised their glasses in acknowledgement, and Cole grinned as he turned to Willow. "As much as I love being back here," he said, "it's you that makes each day matter. I love it when the first rays of sunshine touch your face, and I love falling asleep with you in my arms."

Her cheeks turned red, and she glanced at the others. "Cole, you don't need to—"

"I do. I need to do this in front of the people who matter to me." He walked over to her and went down on one knee, grinning when Willow's eyes widened. "Willow Morgan, these last ten months with you have been the best of my life. I can't live without you. I need you to be mine forever."

Tears glistened in her eyes, and she touched his face. "Cole, I know how you feel. I'm not going anywhere."

"I need to make sure of that." He held up the ring that had been burning in his pocket all evening. "This was my mom's engagement ring, the one my dad picked out for her." He cleared his throat. "I will love you with all my heart, every second, of every day. Will you marry me?"

She dropped to her knees in front of him, tears spilling down her cheeks. "Yes, Cole, of course I will marry you. How could I not? I love you beyond words."

The room broke into resounding cheers, and someone thudded him on the shoulder as Cole took her into his arms, and kissed her. It was the woman in his arms, and the cheers surrounding them that made the moment perfect.

He was home, finally, where he belonged.

About The Author

New York Times and *USA Today* bestselling author Stephanie Rowe is "contemporary romance at its best" (Bex 'N' Books). She's author of more than forty-five novels, and she's a four-time nominee for the RITA® award, the highest award in romance fiction. As an award-winning author, Stephanie has been touching readers' hearts and keeping them spellbound for more than a decade with her contemporary romances, romantic suspense, and paranormal romances.

For more information on Stephanie and her books, visit her on the web at www.stephanierowe.com.

Also by Stephanie Rowe

CONTEMPORARY ROMANCE

MYSTIC ISLAND SERIES
Wrapped Up In You
Your Heart to Mine (Early 2016)

EVER AFTER SERIES
No Knight Needed
Fairytale Not Required
Prince Charming Can Wait

WYOMING REBELS SERIES
A Real Cowboy Never Says No
A Real Cowboy Knows How to Kiss
A Real Cowboy Rides a Motorcycle

PARANORMAL ROMANCE

HEART OF THE SHIFTER SERIES
Dark Wolf Rising
Dark Wolf Unbound (early 2016)

SHADOW GUARDIAN SERIES
Leopard's Kiss (early 2016)

ORDER OF THE BLADE SERIES
Darkness Awakened
Darkness Seduced
Darkness Surrendered
Forever in Darkness
Darkness Reborn
Darkness Arisen
Darkness Unleashed
Inferno of Darkness
Darkness Possessed
Shadows of Darkness
Hunt the Darkness (2016)

NIGHTHUNTER SERIES
Not Quite Dead

ROMANTIC SUSPENSE

ALASKA HEAT SERIES
Ice
Chill
Ghost